# THE
# LAST
# ROMANTIC

# THE
# LAST
# ROMANTIC

*a love story inspired by true events*

MIMI B. MARTINOSKI

# THE LAST ROMANTIC

iUniverse books may be ordered through booksellers or by contacting:

iUniverse
1663 Liberty Drive
Bloomington, IN 47403
www.iuniverse.com
1-800-Authors (1-800-288-4677)

Because of the dynamic nature of the Internet, any web addresses or links contained in this book may have changed since publication and may no longer be valid. The views expressed in this work are solely those of the author and do not necessarily reflect the views of the publisher, and the publisher hereby disclaims any responsibility for them.

Any people depicted in stock imagery provided by Thinkstock are models, and such images are being used for illustrative purposes only. Certain stock imagery © Thinkstock.

ISBN: 978-1-5320-0843-6 (sc)
ISBN: 978-1-5320-0845-0 (hc)
ISBN: 978-1-5320-0844-3 (e)

Library of Congress Control Number: 2016917864

Print information available on the last page.

iUniverse rev. date: 12/29/2016

———— ◆ ◆ ————

*This book is dedicated to my family. My father Kiril, the historian. My mother Mirjana, the dreamer. My sister Loriann, the leader and my late brother Richie, the visionary. The tapestry of my life and my art is far richer for having been interwoven with each of your wisdom and light. Much love and gratitude. Special thank you also to Elspeth and Mitzi, my London family. Both of your unwavering love and support truly helped make this dream possible.*

———— ◆ ◆ ————

*There is a life force within your Soul,*
*seek that life.*
*There is a gem in the mountain of your body, seek that mine.*
*O traveller, if you are in search of that*
*don't look outside, look inside yourself and seek that.*
*~ Rumi*

# *Prelude*

Now and then, when Belinda was reminded of her time in London it was always the Italian Gardens at twilight she was transported to. Late Autumn. Dusk and the pervading darkness always descended early at that time of year. The sound of rushing water was constant. Dying rays danced, shimmered on the surrounding stone balustrade. Swan shadows rippled in blackened fountain water. The familiar scent of decayed leaves, damp earth impregnated the air, perhaps the soul's not too distant memory of where ones human vessel continually returned.

The reminiscence evoked feelings of such joy, innocence and rapture. Seamlessly coalesced with feelings of pain, confusion, bitter and sweet loss. Yet, it would forever remain an unregretted, cherished time for Belinda. Such was one's journey to Love, to oneself.

Such a journey begins in many ways; for Belinda it was not with a triumphant trumpets call, but with a whisper. It was an inexorable stirring, a ceaseless ache in her heart. Then, a question and a creative leap occurred and Love answered. Always.

Divine inspiration, mercifully descended and she finally saw for the first time what had always been there: the path. It patiently waited for her return. Finding the path, for many, was like stumbling upon a secret garden door; ancient, covered in dark welts, beyond mysterious. A door, that one was both compelled and repelled to open.

Spirit's evolutionary urge prevailed and Belinda stepped

onto the path; at once committed. Next, unwavering faith and the promise of devotion, utterly, completely in every sense. What could she expect on such a journey?

Daily vicissitudes and deluges of excitement, passion and exhilaration, equally mingled with gut-wrenching heartache, never-ending uncertainty and tremendous, treacherous ego shattering. Love's journey was never boring.

Needless to say, the faint of heart ought not apply. It was that simple. Or difficult, depending on how one chose to look at it...

# Chapter One

EARLY AUGUST. THE TRAIN ARRIVED INTO THE WHITE brilliance of the station seamlessly, precisely on time. The atmosphere was sharp, vibrant. Those long, hot, languid days of late summer were not present here. Having arrived at their final destination Belinda felt a sense of alertness, expectation. Seasoned commuters, bags collected, had already formed a small, impatient queue to exit. The train slowed, hissed to a stop. The desire for movement was thick, palpable. The doors could not open soon enough. A tall, fair-haired, slender man in a wrinkled tan linen suit loosened his tie. He glanced at his wristwatch, foot tapping the entire time. The anxious ego could only be confined for so long.

At last, the chime sounded. The doors released and passengers poured out. Taking a deep breath, Belinda looked around her. The train car was now empty. She slowly stood, gathered her purse, trench coat and luggage and left the train without looking back. On the platform her being was assaulted by the cacophony of station sounds, mingled with the ebullient energy of this glorious city called London. The frenetic pace, the historic and urban splendor that was perennially Paddington Station.

Ahead of her was an endless expanse of pale, bone grey concrete. Above her were multi-paned, arched skylights. Sunlight flooded the station. Geometric shapes dappled the platform and revealed the Heavens, the collective consciousness's current state of mind. The mood was pre-ordained, long before one stepped outside.

Dense crowds, heaving, in various guises, moved in every direction. A controlled chaos, people going places, things were getting done. Fragments of the mood were grinding, monotonous and endless. Doomed to be repeated again and again. Yet she felt the predominant atmosphere was alive and productive. It was an electrical current that was ready to spark at any moment, if only to connect with the desired outlet. It truly rendered her with the feeling of having arrived somewhere paramount, the epicenter of the Universe.

Belinda's stride was even, purposeful. She wore a pale, silver-grey, cotton sateen travel skirt suit. Beneath the tailored jacket, a sleeveless silk ivory blouse with a high, ruffled collar. A tan trench coat lay draped over her arm.

She lifted her face aloft to the light, smiled and reached up to smooth back, behind her ear a lock of thick, chestnut curly hair. Today it was pulled back into a loose braid, thick as a horse's mane. Wisps framed her face, refusing to be tamed. Her brow was smooth, serene, she exuded warmth yet a sense of quiet strength with each step. There was a restrained confidence in the ease, the gracefulness of her movements and compassion and tenderness in the engaged tilt of her head.

Today Belinda walked with a sound conviction in her heart. There was also a noble confidence in her posture and a poised knowingness gleamed in her eyes. She smiled at the puzzled faces of the passersby left in her wake. Their gazes were ones of perplexed awe. Who was she? What did she know to walk with such confidence their inquisitive glances seemed to ask?

Through her spiritual lens Belinda knew that her presence elicited conflicted emotions in other people's deeper consciousness. Was it just a lofty admiration? Yet why was it mingled with an intrinsic feeling of recognition?

Or were other's just appraising the absolute vision of a heroine walking her destined path? No, she knew there was a deeper truth at play. One that spoke of the actual stirring of their own slumbering hero within, a hero being re-awakened and ignited by Belinda's own heroic presence. For many wisdom teaching's conveyed, on the level of form we were all still one and mere mirrors of and for each other reflecting our inner realities. All of us seeking and projecting our own perceived beliefs, highest ideal, values and aspirational selves outward. Ultimately, seeing and seeking our own value in the reflection of people we admired.

Taking the glances gracefully in stride, Belinda looked straight ahead. She knew this heroine had a very clear purpose for this journey, and a very clear vision for her life going forward. She continued to make her way seamlessly through the crowds. Was she just expert at deftly being able to maneuver her way through the throngs of people, she wondered? Or were the crowds perhaps parting for her? Yes, she knew better. Such was the unity, the symphonic flow one felt when walking their destined path. She knew that not only did doors open and obstacles vanish but movements and moments became seamless and the mind calm and so very, very clear.

Immersed, Belinda felt the oneness with the crowd, viscerally connected to the kaleidoscope of emotions that surrounded and engulfed her. There was joy in a child's uninhibited, innocent laugh. There was utter bliss in the passionate crush of a couple's loving reunion. Yet, in the other direction there was woe, emptiness. She felt the strain, the anxiety in a train station attendant's slumped shoulders, vapid glance. A few feet away there was desolation in the lined face of a lone, painfully thin, elderly man, taking respite on his equally ancient suitcase. Her heart went out to all of them, especially the latter two, she felt their silent suffering deeply.

She yearned to tell them to stop. Stop the madness; let the illusion of isolation and suffering go, for it was simply not real. The self-inflicted pain, it was not real, none of it was real. This sense of fear and separation were self-created cages, made with imaginary bars. For one was never alone, we were all here together, tenderly and eternally connected. Divinely linked by that unifying source called Love. Love was the breath that gave the wholeness of humanity life, meaning and purpose.

Belinda sighed. How had we lost our way, she wondered? At one time such sacred, intrinsic beliefs were a way of life. How had we strayed so far from the scared hymns and teachings of *The Tao Te Ching*, *The Upanishads* and Ancient Greek and Roman philosophers where one did not live in fear but understood that life was friendly and meant to be revered and harmonious? Alas, those were simpler times. Today's world was so complex. Our focus on technology had surmounted our humanity in so many ways. This outward looking, fast-paced society made it so difficult for anyone to be still enough to grasp the inner truth that each of us was whole, loved and far grander than we'd been led to believe. That only Love was real. Only Love would set us free, set us all free from the bondage of the ego's inexorable torment.

Ironically, Belinda also knew there was no need to look further than within oneself. Yes, this source, this creative and endless fountainhead of freedom called Love was always found within you. How utterly splendid that our liberation, our salvation was lovingly and gracefully built into us, she mused. It was not a coincidence. We only needed to quiet the mind and open our heart and simply surrender to Love's peaceful call. What a pity it was that most of us were looking everywhere else for it. Belinda's heart emanated with compassion, she yearned to embrace all of these respected yet un-awakened fellow God's she saw. She was reminded of another wisdom teaching, a credo she held dear.

*"For we are all Gods, walking amongst other God's; therefore act accordingly."*

She passed a tiny card stand. There were black and white greeting cards on display, elegant in their unadorned simplicity. There was an equally elegant, tall and slender Indian shopkeeper, who had attached one of the cards to his cash register, its percipient message for all to see and read,

*Be in this world, but not of it.*

It was a brilliant reminder to remain detached, to release society's implacable fixation with the fallacy of achieving fulfillment through consumption and monetary means. Belinda met the warm, amber eyes of the shopkeeper and smiled. Their gazes locked and held. He smiled back, bowed his head and mouthed the word *Namaste*. She too bowed her head, in respect and silent acknowledgement of that words meaning: *The spirit here recognized and honored the spirit there*. Enlightenment was everywhere, if you wanted – no, chose to see it. Yes, even in a Paddington Station card shop.

The biblical verse *Be in this world but not of it*, pointed to a truth that Belinda intuitively embraced and endeavored to live by despite the ego's continual need to maintain a strong hold on the "me and mine" in this intensely material world. The ancient proverb encouraged and promised to set one free from the preoccupation of a solely physical and material existence.

Moreover, Belinda knew this teaching encouraged her rather to *be* in this moment, live and Love with each breath and yes, also engage fully with all the beauty and bounty this earthly life had to offer, for it was truly ours to explore. But, do not become bound to it or by it. For this led to suffering and would be one's ultimate demise.

If only all of humanity could awaken and see beyond the illusion, she wished, beyond this myopic view of life as full of suffering that people mistook for reality. Truly, one had only to simply pull aside the illusory veil to reveal the delicate, yet ubiquitous truth that existed. Only Love was real.

For Belinda knew, intuitively in her heart, that one's purpose in this life was not to vigorously *get* but rather to benevolently and tenderly *let* that which was within you: one's truth, the Love and light within to harmoniously flow out into one's life and the world, thus igniting others to do the same.

Alas, she also knew one's path to awakening to truth was always unique to the individual and their willingness and thus divinely timed. As were the evolutionary lessons that one would learn from Love along the way. Therefore, such was the distinctive beauty, the joy and the pain we would all encounter on the path. Belinda glanced around her, saw first hand much of the illusion of duality and disparity on display in London's Paddington Station. Illusions arriving in the form of lessons in our personal lives, to be played out over and over again until awakening occurred. Until we finally understood: *How you do anything, is how you do everything.*

Belinda picked up her pace as she continued to weave her way through the crowds. It pleased her to hear snippets of multiple languages, to see the multitudes of ethnicities, many exotic from across the globe. London's proximity, intimacy, with the rest of Europe was viscerally felt and visually evident.

A familiar sense of jubilation, of captivation upon having arrived in this superlative city set in Belinda's heart. Yet this time it was amplified, tenfold. Today, the joy she felt coursing through her own veins flowed in harmony with the city's own magnetic pulse. This trip was different of course therefore it was no surprise to her that each moment vibrated with an acute sense of clarity, corporeal possibilities.

Never before had being in London felt so deeply right to her. Never before had Belinda's life and the raw dynamism of this exceptional city been more real, more thrilling and mellifluous with her entire being. Her heart suddenly expanded, overflowed with an un-nameable feeling, a sense of bliss swept over her.

Belinda yearned to go deep, to let go, to bare her soul and receive all of Love's splendor. Receive its truth and even its wrath, to transcend it all. Forever ecstasy was what she seeked. Belinda was ready for all of it. For the first time she felt truly open, desperate to connect, ready to peel away the egoistic layers of herself and to reveal and surrender to her truth within. All of this only felt possible here in London somehow, outside of her comfort zone. Yet, it was all quite familiar, as though this reckoning were pre-written.

She arrived at the taxi stand. A procession of London's iconic perfectly poised and polished black cabs awaited. She greeted the driver with a playful smile, sending him a silent blessing as her eyes met with his very earnest gaze. He held her gaze, quickly smiled back and then shyly looked away, his cheeks endearingly flaming up. He wore a newsboy cap; his pale blue work shirt was stretched, taut across his robust chest, the sleeves rolled up over thick forearms. She gave him her desired destination and climbed into the back of the car. Belinda observed as he stood, as if transfixed, for a moment. He appeared completely flummoxed by something and it had rendered him motionless. His soulful gaze seemed to reveal, he too felt the sincerity of the moment when their eyes met. *The spirit here recognized the spirit there.* He then smiled and there was a revitalized, euphoric, burst of youthful joy in his step and actions. He began to whistle while he loaded her case into the car and got in behind the wheel. Belinda smiled. *Namaste* did it every time.

Having noticed her accent, he asked where she hailed from, what brought her to his wretched and beloved city?

"I'm Canadian. I'm here to write my first book" was her automatic, succinct reply.

The response surprised Belinda, such conviction. Yes, she repeated to herself, I am here to write my first book. She liked the sound of that immensely.

"Well, fancy that." He replied. "Any room in your story for an English bloke who's been driving a London black cab for nearly thirty years? Boy, could I tell you a story or two love", he replied and laughed heartily.

She smiled, grasped the above handle and braced herself as the car lurched forward and was instantly swallowed up into London's dense traffic.

———◆◆———

Belinda leaned back, peered out the window and relished the afterglow of arrival. London's entire mystique beckoned, its romance, history, its dark and light, its heart and heartache. All of it wooed her from all directions. Everything she cherished in life; creativity, history, integrity, romance, sacred traditions and elegant comportment were heightened, available in copious doses here in London.

The cab turned, the driver decided to give Belinda a more scenic route and cut through Hyde Park. She rolled down the window, the breeze was sweet, carried with it the scent of fresh cut grass. She was rendered nostalgic, transported to childhood summers frolicking and rolling around in the yard with her older sister and younger brother. Leaning her face out the window, she extended her hand feeling the wind between her fingers. The sun peeked in and out of the trees, the wind caressed her hand, moved up her bare arm, trailed up to her cheeks, her lips.

Belinda reached for the end of her braid, she pulled at the band, combed her fingers through her hair and shook her head, unraveled the thick curls and waves. They cascaded down around her shoulders, her back. A sense of freedom, bliss swept over her. Her heart leaped, suddenly each second truly felt ripe for the extraordinary to occur.

———◆———

They were headed to Pimlico Road. Belinda knew the area well. It was a picturesque street with numerous shops, interior décor ateliers, cafés and restaurants. Adding to the area's charm was the bronze statue of Mozart at aged 8. It marked the composer's childhood stay in the area, in 1764, where he had apparently composed his first two symphonies. He stood in Orange Square, on the corner of Ebury Street and Pimlico Road, holding centre court over all the Square's proceedings and adding a dash of playful, impish air.

The area also boasted of one of London's most beloved, rustically romantic French restaurants, its reputation untarnished since it welcomed its first patrons back in 1962. Upon entering one was greeted with the pungent aroma of garlic, wine and cassoulet. Innumerable amounts of faux grapes hung on rusted mesh wire walls and a multitude of straw baskets dangled overhead. The rich terracotta colour palette combined with all the scents and French-speaking staff genuinely evoked the feeling of partaking in an amorous rendezvous in the Provence countryside, not the center of London.

There was also the splendid farmers market that appeared in the square every Saturday morning. Belinda relished watching all the various people converge from around the neighborhood. There was the eccentric, white-haired gentleman who rode in on his rusty bicycle, clad in a newsboy cap with bright mustard-hued corduroy trousers and a worn tweedy brown blazer with one elbow patch missing. There were two elderly ladies, sisters perhaps. Both wore smart floral dresses, pearls and wooly ivory cardigans. There were also the obligatory chic and disheveled young families and their unruly, ruddy-cheeked children running amuck in angelic fair-isle sweaters and bright red Welly's. They squealed with devilish delight as they stained their cherub faces and chubby little hands with fistfuls of berries and homemade chocolate.

All meander about, amongst the stands of abundant, local produce, fish, meat and foul. Wicker baskets overflowed; artisan breads, hand-made jams, bottled milk and newly hatched eggs. The scene was enduring. Belinda was left to ponder what year it really was. These were the moments, she felt, one should treasure. Endlessly and happily repeat. Such was the timelessness, the eternal enchantment of the London Belinda loved anew each time she returned.

The cab came to a stop and brought her back to the present from her reverie. They had arrived. It was nearing the end of the workday, the street busy with commuters. Two handsome chaps were walking by, both in navy suits, starched white shirts, equally somber ties and expressions.

Their immaculately groomed faces, perfectly side-parted hair lent them an austere air, a waxy perfection. Belinda noticed one fellow, trousers cuffed and cropped, sported a pair of brilliant crimson socks. Their red-bloodedness was finally revealed as their pace slowed to glance appreciatively as a slender calf, followed by a cascading crown of pre-Raphaelite chestnut curly hair came out of the car.

The driver, grunting, yet still smiling, placed Belinda's enormous suitcase onto the stoop. She thanked him, clasped his hand with both of hers and handed him a considerable tip for his burden. His eyes beamed, he took her hand, gallantly turned it over, kissed it. He wished her Godspeed on her stay in London, on her book. With a playful wink and the tap of his cap he disappeared into the evening night.

The flat was located on Pimlico Road, south of Sloane Square, off of Lower Sloane Street. Belinda admired the glossy front door; it was painted the most brilliant shade of peacock blue. The curved brass handle gleamed, beckoned. She knelt to fetch the key from underneath the potted plant and then delicately slipped it into the lock, turned the key.

The act was intimate, symbolic. The sound of the lock releasing was bliss to her ears. Access was granted, she smiled, and with it a new chapter in her life began. She confidently pushed the heavy door open and was confronted with a dimly lit vestibule. A long rectangle, faux-damask wallpaper in pale pink draped the walls, corners beginning to peel. In front of her was an expanse of black and white checkerboard tile floor that led to a flight of stairs. They were carpeted in a dusty rose that had surely seen better days. She groaned. There wasn't a lift and her flat was on the third floor. Welcome to London.

———•◆•———

Breathless, after what seemed an eternity of stairs, she finally arrived at her front door. She let herself in, stopped and surveyed the room. Relief. The flat was just as it appeared in the advert, sparse, yet elegant. She parked her luggage and placed her purse, keys and jacket on the console table in the anteroom.

The flat belonged to an elderly, English woman, who spent her summers away, fortunate enough to have a direct escape hatch from the smog of London to the breezy Cote d' Azure, according to the chatty let agent.

Belinda walked about, opened windows, hoping to dispel some of the fug and fusty aroma that lingered in the air. She entered the kitchen. The walls, the cupboards were painted a putrid, pale peach. A turquoise vase with a large bouquet of pink peonies sat on the otherwise bare wooden table. Tucked into the flowers, a welcome note from the letting agent. How thoughtful.

Belinda opened the kitchen window, the night air had turned cool, the busy street at once was very still. She turned around, faced the room. It had gotten quite dark, she should turn on some lights. The solitude of the moment, the encroaching darkness was comforting yet somehow isolating. She did not move. The streetlight had cast a double shadow on the wall in front of her; it gave the illusion of someone else in the room with her. She suddenly wished she did have someone there, to share this moment with. It would make it feel more real, somehow.

She wrapped her arms around herself. Why did she suddenly feel frightened? She turned, seeking comfort, solace in something, anything real, tangible. She made the right decision by coming to London, she told herself, there was no turning back, not now. With that thought she leaned over; eyes closed and buried her face in the soft, buttery bosom of peonies. She gathered the abundant blossoms with both hands, inhaled deeply, repeatedly.

———————

Later, seated in the sitting room, Belinda surveyed the space. The walls were pale yellow, the trim a hi-gloss white. There was a white marble chimneypiece, a gilded clock sat on top. The room's colour palette was a range of anemic green, beige and yellow yet reassuring in its lived-in shabbiness. The English furniture was a polished dark mahogany wood, elegant and timeless. A heavy, pedestal dining table seemed to sigh ponderously in the far corner. A beige linen roll-arm, castor-footed chair and matching, deflated looking sofa dominated the room. Mismatched needlepoint pillows of flowers, dogs were strewn across the sofa. There were sketches of children's profiles, paintings of horses on the walls. All appeared as though they had been in the family for generations. Belinda was drawn to the big window that overlooked a quaint, tree-filled mews in the rear. A lovely oasis from the daily commotion, bustle on Pimlico Road.

The area was truly idyllic, picturesque and yet a stone's throw from the flutter and clamor of Sloane Square, King's Road and Knightsbridge. It was a very charming, very pleasant spot to be letting. Pleasant spot indeed, yet also oddly familiar. Belinda paused. How had she not made the connection sooner? She shook her head at the irony, at herself.

Pray tell, she mused, what was it about the human condition that while apparently yearning for change, something new, one ultimately re-created or somehow found oneself in such similar surroundings, sometimes even the exact replica, of what one wanted escape or a change from?

Perhaps because her discontent, restlessness had less to do with her surroundings or anything external for that matter, and more to do with a deeper, internal and more emotional malaise, she contemplated. How easily we forgot, she noted, that no matter where you go, there you were; you always took yourself and your issues with you. She was reminded of a line from the poem Ithaca,

> *"The Laestrygones and the Cyclopes and furious*
> *Poseidon you will never meet on your journey unless*
> *you drag them with you in your Soul, unless your*
> *Soul raises them up before you..."*

Belinda sighed as she pushed open the sitting room window. The evening air was cool, refreshing. Her ears begun to adjust and take in the jumble of sounds that confronted her. Fragments of conversations, the clatter of crockery and jazz music from a radio all floated over from flats across the way. Londoners were preparing for dinner, just like anywhere else. Belinda found the scenes of domesticity unsettling. It was all too mundane.

What did she expect? A chimerical display of elegant ladies in long satin ruby hued dresses with tiny cinched waists and milky bare shoulders languidly seated in the window smoking cigarettes as their tall debonair and tuxedo clad husbands prepared dirty martinis? Yes, this was London after all. Yet, who were all those people, she wondered? What were their stories, their dreams? All of us in such close proximity, practically within arms reach, yet most she would never see, never meet. It seemed such a pity. Her heart suddenly clenched with anxiety.

In the next moment the soothing rustle of tree leaves

in the wind transported her to sublimity and reminded her of the inner-connectedness of all life. She felt comforted, instantly her being was eased. She moved away from the window. She was suddenly exhausted, completely knackered from the flight, the emotional tumult, the days long journey. She fell back onto the sofa. Putting her feet up she kicked off her pumps and made the executive decision to unpack in the morning.

A long sigh escaped her lips. Out the window she saw the moon above the treetops. Mother-of-pearl-grey, its brow was un-creased, calm. She saw it as the omnipresent eye of Love watching over her, guarding her in her slumber. She felt safe. She smiled and fell instantly into the deep, restful sleep of the weary yet content.

# Chapter Two

THAT NIGHT BELINDA'S DREAMS REVEALED TO HER THE TRUE provenance of this heroic and extraordinary journey. In sleep, as in meditation, her spirit was emancipated from the flesh's constraints to wander the mind's psychological terrain freely. She flitted backward and forward, upward and downward in time and delved deeply into the subconscious waters of her psyche and the why and how this hastened and intrepid dispatch to London came about.

She went back, back to where it all began, and in this case, the tale for Belinda began across the pond in Canada, in a delightful city called Toronto and in an area known as Mount Pleasant.

As its name conveyed, it was quite a pleasant part of the city to live in. The neighborhood abounded with large sweeping trees and lovely houses designed in various architecture. There was the French bakery across the street from her flat. Upon entering the shop checkerboard blue and white cloth covered tables greeted you along with row upon row of warm and crusty baguettes and the most delicate, flaky croissants and patisseries. Best of all was the proprietor; a gentle giant of a French African baker.

One Italian and one Greek restaurant on the same side of the street, both intimate, decades old and still family-run. Antique dealers, along with flower shops, a fine toy store and a gelato café dotted the avenue. There was also, of course, the requisite, archaic art-house movie theatre. The seats were tiny, covered in threadbare velvet and, nostalgically, rocked back and forth. The air was always a bit musty, the wallpaper faded, water-stained, peeling in places but lending the right amount of old-world charm. It was replete with a neon sign out front, eponymously named The Mount Pleasant.

It was all quite indeed perfect. But, having lived there ensconced in all her creature comforts for a few years, Belinda had recently been plagued by the philosophical question of, was it real? Could anything so perfect, so picturesque also be real? To some, and most certainly to the contented spirit, nestling oneself and one's family in such an idyllic and blissful setting could be quite transcendent. Ideally, the conscious spirit engaged in the world's beauty and bounty yet knew to remain detached, unencumbered by these trivial luxuries. For the conscious spirit knew intuitively to,

*Be in this world, but not of it.*

Belinda also knew, the capricious and unconscious person would find such an existence and setting bromidic at best and maledicted, a perpetual purgatory at worst. And yet, even the contented soul, which constantly yearned for creativity was predicated on an inclination to evolve, to claw passionately at such a shiny varnished perfection. Such was the creative spirit's ache for transcendence, gravitas and visceral unadorned truth.

All one had to do was look to nature for evidence of this truth, Belinda thought, for such engineered perfection did not exist as such. Did not a rose also have thorns, she reminded herself? Yes, untouched nature was not manicured magnificence but rather a savage garden with new life growing out of decay and rot.

Toronto was also the city in which Belinda was born. She loved the city, having known and lived there since birth she likened her affection for it to that of an older sibling – one that was comforting, wise and a tad bit over protective at times.

Yet invariably, like many a young bird, one's unbounded spirit eventually had the innate desire to break free, become less comfortable, less protected and feel the thrilling exhilaration of spreading one's wings to soar off with boldness and independence to far, uncertain and exotic locales.

For Belinda this devotional yearning came a little later in life. A life in which Love had dealt her an assorted bouquet of rosy, peak moments and ravishing, velvety romance but also thorny disappointments and withering heartbreak as well. Such was the seeming paradox of life for one not yet fully awakened. Yet even within this illusory paradox Belinda's conviction in Love, albeit quite tenuous in those days, still enabled her to remain optimistic.

Yet, if she were completely honest with herself, she knew Love's gentle promptings went as far back as she could recall. Perpetually vying for her attention, earnestly trying to guide her back to truth.

Alas, free will would make this a most arduous task for Love, time and time again. But, much like the effort of trying to keep a beach ball under water, your true desires would eventually find a way to pop up and command your attention and eventually become your divine decree. As the Upanishad's postulated in India in 800 BCE;

> *You are what your deep, driving desire is.*
> *As your desire is, so is your will.*
> *As your will is, so is your deed.*
> *As your deed is, so is your destiny*

Destiny indeed. Belinda knew she had arrived at a juncture in her life that told of something fundamentally askew in her heart. This made it very clear to Belinda that there was indeed a piece of her life's puzzle that was eluding her and that it required her rapt attention. Post-haste. This quandary prompted her to review her current position.

She was of a confident age, old enough to have gained some wisdom yet young enough to still stumble, albeit a bit more gracefully, once in a while. She was unencumbered, enjoyed a successful, although increasingly disenchanting advertising career and while she adored Toronto, Belinda's spirit also yearned to live, breathe in the air of other lands at some point in her life.

That being said, she knew she would always have a deep bond with Toronto, believing that there was always a reason why you were born in one city over another. An ardent believer and reader of much of the world's wisdom traditions, Belinda held true to the notion which many of them stated that in order for one to truly know where one was meant to go in life, one needed to fully accept and be at peace with where one came from. This aphorism always seemed to calm any anxiety and also lent some desired perspective when daily life would get a little too prosaic for her liking and the urge for a new horizon would become paramount.

And yet, that fateful day seated cross-legged with her back straight on her cognac-hued leather chesterfield sofa Belinda could not help but feel a heaviness in her heart and a deep yearning to be doing something else, somewhere else. She leaned back, her slender frame erect, expectant and took in her surroundings.

What she saw was a beautifully curated flat, with Rococo moldings on buttermilk walls, an impressive chimneypiece and an expanse of gleaming walnut floors. In the air lingered her signature Penhaligon's scent, Artemisia: crisp green apples and nectarines deliciously mingled with jasmine tea, honeyed vanilla, a hint of amber and sensuously rounded out with musk, oak moss and whiff of sandalwood. It was much like how people described Belinda herself; refreshing, warm with a sense of child-like wonder, yet also intense with an old-soul wisdom and sensuality. Full of deep layers all yearning to unfold.

She had moved into the flat less than a year ago and immediately set about turning the innocuous, characterless space into the exquisite manor house she envisioned - and she, its residing Chatelaine.

It was a house filled with beauty and familial heirlooms that also echoed another time, that yearned for a more genteel way of life. Looking around that day Belinda did not feel the usual leap of joy at what she had so meticulously created. What she felt was a sense of accomplished detachment. For something else was whispering to her spirit, hinting that there was something else far grander, far more important to create, to surrender to, connect with.

It also suddenly struck her, how her life aesthetic even reflected a wistful, timeless sensibility of a bygone era. This predilection for antiquity was deeply ingrained. She recalled always being drawn to old things that told a story and older people her entire life. One of her fondest childhood memories was of rainy, summer afternoons where she'd watch endless hours of old black and white films whilst curled up with her mother on the sofa.

Films where gallant heroes and radiant heroines would surmount challenges and hardships with physical, emotional and intellectual aplomb. Yet it was not those heroic figure's moral perfection that fascinated Belinda, albeit worthy of note, it was their flaws, vulnerability, steely integrity, contradiction in character and ultimately their compassion to the human condition, its fragility and suffering, that most touched and inspired her.

It was a heroism that tapped into one's raw, creative energy to overcome the atrophy of humanity's ego. Heroes who rebelled against convention, most certainly the status quo, and reached further, higher and were not bound by society's collective egoistic downward pull of right and wrong doings but in clawing forward, evolving their spirit higher and thus inspiring all of humanity along with them.

A world where honor, integrity, compassion and beauty were the driving forces behind all of life's interactions and endeavors. Those were the fearless archetypes that inspired Belinda as a child and left their indelible mark at so tender an age.

Belinda knew this old world ethos and sense of timelessness had been a constant presence her entire life. It was a light from within her very soul; an enduring ease of *being* and a tenacious desire for authenticity that went far beyond her years. Countless times while growing up she would have people refer to her as an "earnest, warm-hearted child with such an old soul..." Belinda, regardless of her age or where she was or whom she was with exuded a warmth and kindness and was always comfortable in her own skin.

Yet, there was also something else present, a value much loftier than comfort or ease with oneself that was instantly felt in her presence. It was an innocent reverence for life and an exultation of her very essence. It was this reverence for life, for being alive that one felt and was instantly drawn to upon meeting her.

Clues to such proclivities were present everywhere, even in her dress as she favored conservative clothing with an innate sense of relaxed elegance, romanticism, classism, utility, tailoring and heritage. Her style spoke to a respect, an appreciation for the strength, grace and simple beauty of the human form.

All of this conservatism in style was balanced out, by nature no less, with two distinctive features that perpetually conveyed a sense of playfulness, whimsy and ebullient warmth upon meeting Belinda. The first was a lustrous mane of thick, unruly, curly chestnut hair. It framed her face and fell in long, silken tendrils half way down her back. That was, it did when it wasn't tamed back in a long braid like it was that day and most days. The second was a full sensual mouth, ripe as a plum. Lips that were full, soft and found it effortless to smile easily and often.

Looking to the wall on her left, she saw the framed heirloom needlepoint art-work and smiled at its familiarity. While the flat's surface was reminiscent of a French Chateau-cum-English Manor a more discerning eye could ascertain various Eastern European influences, as Belinda's parent's provenance harkened from Macedonia, the former Republic of Yugoslavia. Others quickly discerned that Belinda had a very unique approach to life and the art of living.

Belinda's glance moved on to her mantle-piece. She smiled at the array of miss-matched framed photographs of family and friends. Toronto also held the people she loved most and could count on. Could she move away from them and actually be happy?

She knew she took for granted their current proximity. Currently, access to unconditional love and support was only a tube ride away. How would she fare if an entire ocean separated them? Her family would always prefer to have her near by but they would also never hold her back if there was something she truly wanted to experience in her life. Leaving them would definitely be an emotional gamble. Was it a gamble she was willing to take? She let the thought sink in, waited to see what feelings it elicited. Any reservations or feelings of fear were still over-ridden by a nagging feeling of ennui, of inexorable discontent. What, pray-tell was really going on here? What was she missing? What root desire was being blocked?

True, she had yet to meet the man of her dreams, a noble hero equal to her resplendent heroine. But this fact, epic as it may have been for an ardent romantic such as Belinda, it was still secondary to her heart's overall feeling of discord. What was next for her? Moreover, what did she want right now? If she could wave the proverbial magic wand, what would be her heart's desire in this present moment?

———•———

The dream then showed the days that followed, those pivotal days of awakening and all were full of fervent, earnest reflection. There was endless meditation and intermittent frustration with vagarious thoughts racing through her mind. Ultimately, it wasn't until there was complete, utter surrender to this monumental quandary that inspiration mercifully struck.

It was a regular day, she was again seated on her chesterfield sofa, completely calm, having just come out of a meditation session when *it* came suddenly and with such liberating clarity. Belinda instantly knew if she could have her most vivid, romantic and creative hearts desire come true, she knew she wanted to follow through on a creative passion that had been beckoning for years.

A creative passion that had been nipping at her heels but she'd never given it any serious consideration or permission to fully surface, until now. Belinda wanted to write. No, she knew she must write. She didn't know what she would write but knew this call to write had to be explored by her.

The writing seed had been planted long ago, at the tender age of seventeen. Belinda's English Literature teacher had pulled her aside just before graduation and told her that she needed to be a writer. Yes, her teacher said very firmly, Belinda must pursue a career in writing. She recalled how much those words had terrified and excited her. She knew she loved to read, voraciously so, and that writing in school had always come easily but she didn't see her self as a writer, or an artist for that matter. Moreover, she didn't relate at all to her idea of what the writer archetype looked like. Introverted, broody and quite tortured with dark thoughts and equally dark inclinations.

Belinda was popular, out-going, friendly and happy, an optimistic person at heart. Plus, her ease and comfort with writing made her always take it for granted. Wasn't your vocation supposed to be something you found arduous and challenging? Something one had to really work at and even mildly disliked and wanted to escape from? Surely that was how she observed the role models around her felt about their jobs. Work was just that, work. Such naiveté, how had such faulty thinking become so ingrained in her subconscious? Regardless, that day the seed had indeed been firmly planted and was left in abeyance to germinate and sprout at the exact right moment.

That moment was today. With this unleashed awareness came further inspiration. Belinda also knew instantly, with further certainty the exact setting for her story. She'd had an immediate affinity, an on-going love affair with a particular city for years. She'd made numerous sojourns, had always yearned to experience living there yet never found the time nor the opportunity to make it happen, until now. Such divine inspiration brought with it clarity, conviction and a heady dose of excitement. Which, in turn, prompted swift and inspired action.

Belinda, being quite resolute when she decided on something, set out on implementing her plan in the days that followed. She quit her job, let her flat, withdrew the necessary savings, bid adieu to her beloved family, friends and emotionally readied herself to embark on an unknown compulsion to one of the world's most superlative and literary cities across the Atlantic Ocean and ultimately to the charming little flat, with a peacock blue door on Pimlico Road.

She smiled in her sleep, for she now knew and understood that when the spirits call beckoned one had to act, if only guided by and trusting in the intuitive certainty that a grand destiny awaited.

# Chapter Three

LONDON RECEIVED BELINDA INTO ITS FOLD JOYOUSLY, wantonly. *Love a city and it would surely Love you back*. Mornings she was to be found writing from the café down the street from the flat. Past Buttercup Drycleaners, the Chinese restaurant and Blenheim's Fine Carpet Store.

Belinda always arrived early, claimed her preferred perch at the front window. People watching in London endlessly invigorated her. Her favourites were the tradesmen, filing in and out of their white vans, smiling, amiable. Some English, some Polish and a few other accents she could not place. They were perpetually playful, always ready with a wink and a flirt, their painter's whites splattered in Pollock-esque flair.

Hours of writing ensued, the outpour was endless. She took a break at noon, arched her back, stretched her neck from side to side and relaxed her shoulders. The seat was warm on the bottom of her bare thighs. Her writing uniform, and most days, was well-worn oxford shirts in various faded summer hues or pinstripes of pink, blue, yellow or white and cotton or linen shorts. A lightweight wooly cable sweater or cardigan was tossed over the back of her chair and ballet flats or espadrilles lay discarded on the floor as she preferred being barefoot when writing. There was always a large cup of English Breakfast tea within arms reach, a crumpled FT Arts & Life section lay off to the side to read at luncheon and dog-eared and underlined copies of *Letter's to a Young Poet*, *The Tao Te Ching*, Homer's *The Odyssey*, *Brideshead Revisited*, John Keats poems and a book on Rodin's life. These were Belinda's literary and philosophical bibles.

Other days it was a different locale, the same scene yet different cafés, in neighboring areas. Indulgent Kings Road, bustling, burnt red brick-hued Knightsbridge, chic, cobblestoned streets of Marylebone, the elegance of Mayfair or the pastel, whimsical splendor of Notting Hill.

Inspiration was everywhere. The light in London was phenomenal. Each sunset a Turner painting, at once moody, violet, pearly grey and then pale yellows, misty greens and dusty roses. Victorian, Edwardian, Tudor building facades covered with the patina of age and city soot, rain stained churches intermingled with contemporary buildings. She loved the graphic, bold, white stripe crosswalks on black asphalt, elegantly referred to as "zebra crossings".

Intriguing also were the old black lacquered lampposts on certain streets in Mayfair with carriage lights and a very familiar, gold embossed double C. Some sleuthing revealed it was perhaps the enduring and utterly romantic gesture of Bendor Grosvenor, the 2nd Duke of Westminster to none other than Coco Chanel and their secret affair in 1923. It all fascinated. London's secrets, its sentiment and romantic mystique was unending.

Although her Canadian accent instantly set her apart, Belinda's creative spirit, adoration of the city, its inhabitants instantly beguiled and captivated them. As Oscar Wilde once said: *"Talk to every woman as if you loved her, and to every man as if he loved you and you will have the reputation of possessing the most perfect social tact."*

---

The writing was prolific in those early days. She wrote with fervor, an ardent outpouring of earnest, raw emotion.

Reams of pages filled with luminous, unselfconscious, heartfelt prose of her current sate of mind, of her London life, the places, the mood, the people she saw and met.

The words flowed from her, profusely, copiously. There were times when she was not sure if she was writing or if the story was being written for her. Most certainly she was aware of that other force, her creative spirit. The spirit that was constantly witnessing everything, that animated one's mind and body.

Many a time when writing Belinda would feel such a connection to spirit, it's flow and that her hands and fingers were mere conduits for a spirit seeking a release, an outlet to manifest its creative expression into existence. During those exquisite moments, her heart overflowed, transcended, she entered another dimension. Time did not exist.

At the end of the day, Belinda returned to the flat deliciously spent, satiated. She desired nothing. She peered at herself in the mirror. Her skin was flushed, iridescent. There was an ethereal glow, a sense of wonder and innocence in her eyes. She was as she was at five years of age. She was transformed into her child-like self. She smiled at her reflection. She had discovered the fountain of youth in her artist-hood.

Alas, even as optimistic and positive as Belinda was in those early weeks she would still fall prey to the ego's bouts of doubt, melancholy and that eternal human condition known as impatience. Impatience for what, she would always ask herself, yet knew the answer was the end of uncertainty of course. She also knew it was one of life's eternal and most futile preoccupations but that knowing did not absolve her from the ego's lusty grasp.

It was late August, a cool summer's evening. Belinda sat cupping a steaming cup of tea by the large window in the sitting room. She wore a long ivory cashmere robe and sat sideways; her bare legs were thrown insouciantly over one arm of the chair, her right foot restlessly tapped at the air. She sipped and stared out onto the little mews as the full weight of such odious emotions began to descend upon her unsuspecting shoulders. They landed, like an opaque web, all around her, clouding her inner vision. The weight quickly turned oppressive.

She tilted her head to either side, stretched her neck, trying to shake the dreadful anxiety beginning to mount. Pray-tell, what was going on, she wondered? Was it perhaps homesickness? Or had the novelty of living in London begun to fade, as it was wont to do when routine set in? She felt in a moribund state, a sense of dread, suddenly fearful. The chirping birds had gone, replaced by a child's incessant cry from across the way. On and on it went, wailing, maddening. Her heart beat faster. She stood, closed the window and sat on the sofa, eyes closed, focusing on her breathing.

She needed to steady herself. She had made the right decision by coming to London. She'd never been happier than in the last few weeks. Her mind raced to recall the initial excitement, the seemingly endless supply of confidence, of joy at the onset of this journey.

Such conviction. She desperately needed a heavy dose of that right now. Belinda's mind went back, back to the days just before she was to depart for London. The certainty in her decision was so clear then. Her spirit's whispered encouragement was ubiquitous. An extraordinary journey awaited, the rustling trees seemed to say. Far grander than one can imagine, was the wind's caress. A journey that would unequivocally change her life forever, promised the winking evening stars.

Noted, she had armed herself with a steely resolution, an open heart to see this adventure through come what may and added a few love charms for good measure. Yes, the charms, her talismans, meant as reminders that if she were faithful to Love, to her path in life, she really would be living the life of her dreams.

It was Belinda's intrinsic belief that living the life of your dreams would also ultimately lead to meeting the person of your dreams. It only made sense.

*Trust that which you seek, was also seeking you.*

She recalled the day before she was due to leave for London. She saw herself again, in her bedroom. Her bed, hardly visible, was covered in mounds of clothes. It seemed to groan from the sheer weight of her enormous suitcase. Did she need all of this stuff? Really? When had she accumulated all of it? A sense of revulsion set in. She stood, looked around the room. The walls were a velvety, overcoat grey colour. Rococo paneled walls, like loving arms that encircled her head as she slept.

Above the bed, in a gilded frame, was a majestic painting of white magnolias in repose. The dark, dramatic backdrop offset the delicate ivory petals, lent the painting a sensual, moody air. The magnolia flower symbolism suddenly confronted her: beauty, dignity, nobility and perseverance if she recalled correctly. Ah perseverance indeed, she murmured to herself. She could use a dose or two of that virtuous elixir right now. Her glance returned to the melee on her bed, the visual reality of what she was about to do fully struck her.

Had she really made the decision to pack up her life

and go live in London? Really? A wave of fear, uncertainty flooded her being. She was really doing this. Had she gone mad? Was she, perhaps, experiencing some sort of early mid-life crisis? Had she actually quit her job, rented her flat to go write in London, England? Really?

Right now the notion sounded less so boldly heroic, creative and enduringly romantic and more so idealistic, utterly naïve and completely grandiose. Perhaps she failed miserably as a writer? What made her think that she'd actually be able to write anything of value or benefit to the world for that matter? Who did she think she was? And what, pray-tell, came next? She'd quit her job. There was no work, no career to return to. She must be absolutely mad to have done this.

She was suddenly on an emotional balance beam. Teetering, the familiar pull of fear, anxiety beckoned her to topple on either side. Her heart started to pound. Belinda struggled to steady herself, but her limbs had become heavy, cement-like. A lead weight descended upon her chest, it was difficult to breathe. The clock ticking on her bedside became amplified, deafening. Sirens blared on the street outside.

Her emotional resolve was dissipating quickly, like sap from a tree it was being wantonly sucked out of her against her will. She realized she was holding her breath. She tried to take a deep breath, but it caught in her throat. Her hand quickly reached up to her neck. It was there her fingers landed on the cool, metal of her necklace. Just as instantly as the fear and the anxiety had sprung up, it was vanquished. Belinda's hand remained at her neck, caressing the charm.

Yes, *this* was why she was doing this. *This* was what was really important. She had recently re-discovered the charm. All tangled, in the back corner of her jewel case. She'd bought it years ago, a mere romantic whim, or so she'd thought. It had caught her eye instantly in the jewelry boutique glass case, stirring something deep within her. She had approached, drawn in by it. She recalled leaning her face down, so close her breath fogged the glass counter. She needed to get closer to it, much closer. It lay, perfectly nestled in green velvet, glinting, shimmering in the light. It was unlike anything she'd ever seen.

A tiny charm, so simple, yet monumental in its meaning. It was of a man and a woman, kneeling before each other, heads bowed, hands clasped. The unmitigated sensuality, the sacredness of their stance, sent a jolt straight to her loins. Two lovers in complete, utter surrender to each other, to Love. The superlative embodiment of two souls kneeling before each other, raw, naked and honoring each other as equals. Each figure was recognizing and paying homage to the heroic in each other. It was Love's essence, fashioned into gold. Belinda knew she must possess it.

———•◆•———

Later back at her Toronto flat, before the mirror, she slipped the charm onto a fine, box-link gold chain. Her eyes remained locked with her reflection. In the next moment she was outside of herself, watching, witnessing the vessel of her being. She watched herself as she tied her hair up, away from her face, neck and fastened the clasp. She held her breath and leaned in, her nose only inches from the mirror. The charm rested right where her clavicle bones met, in that perfect little dip. Belinda watched as her form pressed the charm into her skin. Harder, wanting to brand its meaning into her flesh. She exhaled. Suddenly she was back, inside of herself, looking at the red imprint on her tender skin. The ritual was complete.

———••·•———

Pray-tell, what had happened, she now asked herself? How had such a sacred charm and moment of true providence ended up relegated, a tangled mess, at the back of her jewel case? There must have been a lapse in faith. A weak moment in Love's ardent and infinite truth had surely occurred. It did not matter, the fortuitous reunion, right before she left for London no less, was pre-written.

Belinda had desired a symbol of devotion for this journey, a token to honor the renaissance of her faith in her creative spirit and in true Love. The charm exemplified honoring the heroic not only in her Beloved, but a vow to honor her own heroic spirit and path in life.

Going forward the only notions she would allow to consume her thoughts, her being, were in the milieu of truth, Love, creativity and compassion. A life that revered purpose, meaning and beauty was the life she envisioned. Thoughts, words, deeds and relationships, only those that had the perpetual evolution of her creative spirit in mind would quench, suffice her being. As she donned the necklace for the second time, Belinda made a new vow.

She vowed she would not remove the necklace until she was united and connected with her spirit's romantic equal, her Beloved. It was a Love that she knew would enhance her life by his very own being, a Love that yearned to join and grow in creative and passionate surrender. A Love, her heart whispered, that was also seeking her.

The other charm, a silver stone, was the size of a dollar coin. The words *I love you* artfully etched into it. It had been a sweet gift by an old friend. Belinda carried the stone with her always, now and then caressing the smooth, cool surface. A constant reminder that coming from a place of

Love, in any situation, would always have the most desired and efficacious outcome.

This virtuous ethos and belief in Love came very naturally to Belinda. It was an innate trust. It was threaded through ever fiber of her being, part of her make-up. It had been trying at times. Her life, like most, had not been without tribulations. But this solid foundation in Love, this inexorable sense of optimism always remained steadfast.

The belief that she was meant to live a heroic, wondrous life was constant. Asked, she could hardly articulate its genesis, it seemed to come from that eternal, diaphanous place that always was, always would be within; her spirit. It flourished as she grew older, she felt, knew, from very early on that one was meant to truly *live* life. That to thrive and work from her noblest and best self was the point, not merely existing. Her life, as she chose to view it, was an on-going honorable and romantic adventure and she its ever confident, radiant heroine.

It was this archetypal symbol, the symbol of the heroine, which Belinda most related to and assigned to guide her then and now on this most magnificent return to her true path. She knew even at a tender age this belief would sustain her as a moral compass when life's trappings would want to sway or engulf her whole.

Envisioning herself this way ignited her spirit with exuberance, a passion for life that could only be described as intoxicating. It also injected a heavy dose of confidence, self-respect to stay true to herself, her path and her hero. It was particularly supportive on those long, bleak seeming stretches of time when she would sometimes wonder if she would ever meet this hero, equal to her heroine.

At times frustrated, there didn't seem to be a shortage of men in the world but there did appear to be a shortage of men with the innate confidence, compassion and brilliance Belinda knew were inherent in her hero. She wondered why so few others felt or believed in the grandness of their spirit, that they too were the heroes of their very own passionate Love stories. For, as long as Belinda could recall, she'd felt the essence of a great Love in her life. This feeling was so visceral, so potent at times she would converse with it in private moments, clasp its hand while out for solitary evening walks and bid it goodnight before falling asleep. She knew and found great consolation in the fact that this Love would one day materialize in the flesh when the moment was right.

Therefore, this decision to finally act on her heart's persistent promptings, nurture a creative talent and depart to the city of her dreams was actually a culmination of all the yearnings, pursuits and aspirations Belinda had felt and experienced prior to this moment. It was though all her past life choices had prepared her for this one superlative moment in her life.

The next day, she was boarding the plane. The queue was filled with splendid English accents. Belinda smiled to herself, felt a wave of pure joy spread through her being. Settled into her seat, she slid open the window panel. The long tarmac, shimmering in the sunlight as though paved in black diamonds, seemed to stretch out to infinity.

Belinda took a deep breath. She was embarking on an extraordinary journey laden with much uncertainty, and whilst it was only natural to be completely terrified, Belinda trusted that her faith in Love and its marvelous, pansophic workings would always guide her in the right direction.

She braced herself as the plane started down the runway. In anticipation of take off, she leaned her head back, closed her eyes and told herself as long as she was calm, present, communed daily with Love and heeded the sign posts and the coincidences along the way she would not, could not go astray.

As if to confirm the profundity of her emotions, the plane's powerful jets kicked in at that exact moment, propelling the craft, boldly, seamlessly into its ascent into the sky.

———◆◆———

Coming back to the present and the flat on Pimlico Road, Belinda wondered why it was so hard to reconnect with all that conviction. Why had all those jubilant emotions dissipated? What was this nagging anxiety in her heart? She needed to find a way to reengage with that all powerful and unbounded reserve of spiritual fortitude, confidence and bliss that she'd felt at the onset of this journey.

She decided to set out for a walk, hoping the fresh air would obliterate the malevolent voices in her head and free herself from the thick, swampy doubts that persisted in dragging her mind and heart down, deep into the muck.

———◆◆———

The evening air was instantly uplifting, being outdoors subdued much of the ghastly apprehension in her heart. Belinda headed towards Sloane Square fountain. It was only late August yet already she could discern the musky, decayed scent of autumn in the air. The sun was beginning to set and storefronts were suddenly being illuminated, one by one as she walked past.

Approaching Sloane Square, she heard the perennial rush of the fountain's waterfall. Its constancy always evoked a sense of nostalgia, comfort in Belinda's being. She could not recall a time when the fountain, which depicted the kneeling figure of the Goddess of Love in bronze, was not eternally pouring water from her conch shell.

The Goddess sat atop a large bronze vase-shaped basin, within an octagonal-shaped pool that was intricately lined with pale blue ceramic tiles. Belinda paused for a moment, to commune with Venus. She stood there; still, eyes closed and didn't fight her tangle of emotions. She breathed deeply, eyes still closed, trying to feel, then release the doubt, the anxiety. Opening her eyes, Venus's serene, knowing expression seemed to tacitly convey something to her. Suddenly Belinda was inspired. She reached into her pocket and holding one pence tightly to her heart she silently wished,

"May I always succeed at what I set out to do."

She then tossed the coin into the fountain. After a few more conscious breaths, feeling more centered and calm, she continued walking up Sloane Street with no particular destination in mind. It was a Sunday evening and the streets were desolate, forlorn in their solitude, despite it being one of London's more affluent shopping and walking promenades.

Still somewhat on edge and in need of further reassurance Belinda decided to ask Love for its salient guidance. Being a deeply intuitive person Belinda was heartened by the belief that coincidences were small miracles, purposefully placed in your path and meant to help guide you on the journey in this life.

Had she been wrong in coming to London? If not, why was her being so suddenly wrought with so much anxiety, uncertainty? Was this her true course? Why the compulsion to come to London of all places? Why had she known instantly that it would be the setting for her story? Was this whole trip pre-ordained? Was there perhaps another more exalted reason she was compelled to come here?

Or could it be her one true Love was here, that their combined desire to unite was so powerful that it had actually lured her here? The thought put a bemused smile on Belinda's lips. A romantic notion for sure, but one she truly believed could also be true. She needed a sign, something to confirm that she was indeed on the right path. As she walked she closed her eyes, breathed in deeply. So many questions, how does one choose? But one question surmounted the rest, she found herself tacitly asking,

"Is the man of my dreams in London?"

She opened her eyes. She didn't see anything particularly interesting but she waited, expectantly, knowing her sign was coming. Belinda knew that when you asked Love a question, it would always garner a creative response. Be still, be patient but most importantly be alert, for blink and you would surely miss it.

And then, there it was suddenly, irrevocably. It was a scent, a men's cologne. It wafted over her as she walked. She breathed it in deeply. It carried with it notes of citrus, lavender, balmy spices, pine and a hint of woody musk. Belinda recognized the scent instantly. It stopped her mid stride, she went to sit at a nearby bench, needed to access, ponder its significance.

The cologne she knew very well indeed. But, alas therein lay the irksome quandary. The scent conjured up a twofold association for Belinda. A man she had dated briefly, years ago, had worn that scent, she had taken a liking to it instantly. But, while she had adored his scent the gentleman in question eventually revealed that the few vestiges of hero-like qualities Belinda had gleaned in him upon meeting had actually only been a façade. He had been somewhat older, quite debonair but the manner in which he presented himself turned out to merely be a guise for a very unscrupulous nature and a spurious past. Predictably, and thankfully, the romance had ended amicably, and more importantly, swiftly.

Having always been quite discerning when it came to romance, Belinda had found the whole experience an interesting lesson. Notable also was the fact that the romance had, from the outset, come with an incessant discomfort in Belinda's heart. Looking back, she was able to ascertain that all along her heart had been warning her that the gentleman, the situation had not been in her best interest.

But why that scent in this context? Was it a warning? Or was it a clue to help her recognize the man of her dreams when she met him? She wished the sign would of been clearer. Frustrated and annoyed she shook her head and decided to put it aside for now.

She rose wearily from the bench, she felt emotionally exhausted and turned to head back to the flat; visions of a cup of tea and having a long hot bath eased her mind. As she started back down Sloane Street, Belinda recalled again the scent, the sensual, musky notes. Ah, Love, she mused, its fascinating and intricate workings would never cease to flummox and enthrall her.

Suddenly, a shiver caught hold of her. She pulled up the collar on her navy, quilted jacket, dug her hands into her pockets and picked up her pace. But try as she may, she could not shake the ominous feeling suddenly overcoming her or the icy chill that snaked down her spine.

# Chapter Four

THE NEXT FEW DAYS SEEMED TO BLEND, BLUR INTO EACH other with an outpouring of writing and creative verve. During which time was not a factor for Belinda, she existed in a realm beyond or in-between time. It was a sense of oneness, a heightened consciousness, sensitivity to moments and feelings not minutes ensued. Where ideas, inspiration, queries came and in the next moment they were answered, spontaneously, unfailingly. Surrender was key. She must surrender to the process. Intuitively, she knew this age-old process was very simple. Ancient wisdom teachings confirmed it and Rudyard Kipling coined it well: *drift, wait and obey.*

It was in those sacred creative moments, moments Belinda completely trusted in, that she felt most inspired, most free. They were moments of pure heightened awareness. She felt a deep connection with nature. Her artistry, in full creative bloom, was completely synchronized with nature and universal rhythms. It was on nature's clock, if any, that her artist within thrived. She rose with the sun, creation instantly on the mind. Writing until famished at noon ensued. Mid-afternoon would come and she went for a walk. The desire to commune, breathe with nature in a park and then back at it. All were par for the course. The days, the weeks went by splendidly, ferociously, productively and full of creative vivacity and proliferation.

The flurry of writing was intermingled with the occasional indulgence with mates during the week. They would catch the latest art-house film at the local Curzon. Met for drinks at Claridge's Bar, The Goring or The Library Bar at The Lanesborough Hotel. Exhibits at Tate Modern, the National, Saatchi Gallery and the Wallace a must. Hearty brunches of farm fresh scrambled eggs, in-house smoked salmon at Daylesford on Pimlico or a high tea at The Wolseley or Durrants Hotel with her best London chum. There were also the splendid Sunday morning chamber music concerts at Wigmore Hall that delighted the soul with a dear elderly friend who at almost ninety was still quick as a whip. There was more, much more. All of them exorbitant profligacies, yet all of it inculcated Belinda into London's artistic ethos. It was a culture circuit that was glorious, rigorous and un-yielding.

One evening, a multitude of weeks later, Belinda was due to meet two of her mates, both Canadian ex-pat's now residing in London, at her favourite London restaurant. As she was dressing, Belinda felt a sense of anxious expectation. She knew something special yet ineffable was going to happen that night. She felt it deeply, in the marrow of her bones. She was giddy, her movements clumsy and distracted. She bumped into the dresser, almost dropped her gold love-knot earring down the sink drain. She barely had the patience to dress. What was this odd mélange of feelings, she wondered? She left the flat. She smiled at the pleasant click-clack sound of her black patent Mary-Jane heels made on the checkerboard tile, how it echoed like a tap dance number throughout the vestibule.

She glanced at herself in the long hallway mirror as she walked passed, did a double take. Had her reflection just winked at her? What the devil was going on, she wondered again. Belinda opened the front door, walked to the end of the sidewalk. Just as she was about to raise her hand to hail a black cab, one came to a halt right in front of her. Well, that's an auspicious start to any evening, she said to herself with a smile and climbed in.

The odd sense of prescience was only heightened as her cab pulled up to the restaurants facade. The doorman approached, he was dapperly dressed in the signature green top hat and tails. The polished brass buttons on his coat jacket glinted in the night, as he gallantly opened her cab door with one hand then swooped back to also open the restaurant front door with the other.

She stepped into the restaurant and stopped to soak up her surroundings. How she adored this restaurant. It's dedication to British old world comportment, charm, intimate ambience and artistic heritage was par excellence. The marvelous wood-paneled walls turn the space inward. Sumptuous, emerald-green leather banquettes hugged the outer corners of the walls. Dinner tables were swathed in pristine, white, padded cotton cloth. Windows, covered in opaque white and multi-hued diamond-shaped stained glass, lent a timelessness air to the space. The result was an enchanting quality, it rendered one useless in estimating what time of day, or season it was whilst inside.

Belinda was the first to arrive. Escorted to their table, she slipped into the smooth leather banquette, seated herself to face the entire restaurant. A pale green, cotton napkin with the restaurants embroidered logo was laid elegantly upon her lap. She could suddenly feel there was a perceptible shift in the molecules in the room.

The hair on the back of her neck stood up, suddenly

she knew she was being watched. She ordered a glass of champagne, picked up the menu whilst demurely trying to scan the room. This feeling, of being watched by some unknown audience, intrigued and excited her. The anticipation was like a live electrical current that was hanging in the air. It beckoned to make contact, to connect, release its pent up charge.

Her friends arrived. Kisses, heaps of catching up ensued. The restaurant was alive and buzzing. Each table was occupied, many by London's theatre and intellectual cognoscenti. Intermittently Belinda would again casually scan the restaurant, looking for the source, knowing she would recognize it when she saw it. Main courses arrived. All senses primordially shift to the sizzling feast of steak, fish and that famous Shepherd's Pie displayed before them. They all paused, smiled, prepared to gormandize London with relish.

Belinda raised her fork to her mouth, when suddenly the room took on the sense of moving in slow motion. She paused, fork mid-way, hanging in the air. Voices faded out. Sounds became isolated, heightened. To her left; a champagne cork popped, bubbles fizzed as the bottle overflowed with foam. To her right; a woman's deep throaty laughter followed by cutlery that grated against fine bone china. A camera flashed. A whoosh of wind from the door; the candles at their table were blown out.

Belinda was suddenly compelled to look up. In that moment she met the very precise, exacting, brilliant-eyed gaze of a tall, very handsome, bearded Fellow walking by. Their gazes locked. The hold felt eternal.

His gaze, framed by black spectacles, was concentrated on her, knowing. His lips curled up into a one-sided smile, bordered on being smug. His brilliant eyes flashed, penetrated her to the very core of her being. Belinda leaned back. Her breath was knocked out of her. She blinked, wondered,

"Do I know him?"

He wore a smartly tailored black suit with ivory pinstripes. His gold tie was expertly knotted and his upright posture and perfectly groomed beard lent him an aristocratic air. And then, he was gone. Belinda took another breath. She was completely flummoxed by what had just passed between her and this elegant stranger.

Her companions had not noticed the exchange. Belinda tried to focus on the conversation. Hours seemed to turn into minutes. Their pudding arrived. The sugary sweet scent of Sticky Toffee Pudding filled her nostrils as a long shadow darkened their table. Belinda looked up. It was the Fellow with the brilliant eyes. He stood at their table, his eyes gleamed, locked on her, seemed to dance like fire behind his spectacles. His smile, bemused, was softer more relaxed now.

He introduced himself, he worked with the restaurant, he explained, wanted to ensure they were having a splendid evening and enjoying their dinner. He would also like to personally invite them upstairs to their exclusive members club for a cocktail afterwards. He promised to return to collect them once they were done with their pudding. He smiled and without waiting for their response, met Belinda's gaze once again and turned on his heel and vanished.

Had he just winked at her? Upon closer inspection he was, indeed, quite tall, extraordinarily dashing and his crisp English accent utterly beguiling. Belinda and her dinner companions for that matter were instantly transfixed and only too delighted to oblige his invitation.

Belinda straightened her posture, smoothed her hair back behind her ear. She tried to feign an air of nonchalance at the whole episode as she turned to meet the knowing glances of her mates. It was obvious they too could not help but notice his very focused area of interest. She blushed, innocently shrugged her shoulders in response to the pair of raised eyebrows that confronted her.

———◆◆◆———

The club upstairs was a sensual, laid-back version of the restaurant below. A long, glittering bar held court. Low, cushy club chairs in muted tones of brown, green, mustard and maroon beckoned being sunk into. Numerous luxurious, aged leather sofas were scattered about. The Fellow seated them at a table near the slick, black grand piano. The pianist was playing Tiny Dancer..."Oh how it feels so real... Lying here with no one near... Only you and you can hear me, when I say softly slowly..."

They sat in a circle as the Fellow urbanely chatted about the praises, the perks of the restaurant and a membership at the club. He ostensibly answered Belinda's mate's questions, whilst sending very measured glances at her. She sat back silent, observed mostly. The next hour was a haze. This Fellow was having the oddest affect on her. It was different from anything else she had ever experienced in terms of a male-female dynamic. It was more heightened, transcended gender. It was not Love at first sight, nor was it lust at first sight. It was something else, chemistry she could not name and it involved a unique mix of alluringly foreign, yet viscerally familiar. All jumbled into one.

She found him very attractive. His features were fine, delicate but combined with the virility of his hirsute beard it lent his pulchritude an ethereal, epicene quality. Belinda was also drawn to the ease, the comfort he had in his own skin. He sat leaning back, the club chair appeared diminutive, incongruous to his long, sinewy limbs, which were splayed out gracefully before him. One leg was bent at the knee, the other with his ankle resting on the opposite knee. His elbows rested on the arms of the chair as he gestured with long, elegant fingers as he spoke.

There was something else about his essence, or their combined chemistry that continued to transfix, to elude her, and much to Belinda's frustration she could not put her finger on what it was. She was unaccustomed to this feeling. She knew she was definitely out of her romantic milieu with this Fellow, but it also excited her. She continued to observe whilst the others chatted.

Now and then, when their eyes meet, Belinda was overcome again by an illusory feeling of intense propinquity and intimacy. She blushed, absently raised her glass to her lips and looked away. It was only when the group stepped out for a breath of fresh air did she gain some longed for insight.

The rooftop terrace was moon-drenched and painfully tiny. Literally, there was only room enough for ten people. The Fellow very gallantly opened the door for her, stepped past her to make room for the others, and chose to stand directly in front of Belinda. It was in that exact moment, when he very intimately slid past her, that an eerily familiar scent wafted over her. Belinda froze. His cologne, its scent and the profundity of it hit her instantly.

Her mind went into a tailspin. She knew that scent. She was transported back to that evening on Sloane Street; over a month ago now, when in her melancholic state she had asked Love if the man of her dreams was in London. She was given a sign, it came in the form of a scent, a men's cologne and call her mad but it smelled exactly like the very cologne this Fellow was wearing. She would bet her life on it.

Belinda felt the tiny terrace starting to expand. What did this mean? Was this a sign to help her recognize something special about this Fellow? Yet, there was also a dull nagging sensation, a feeling that she was forgetting something significant. She figured it couldn't be too important if she could not recall it and pushed it out of her mind. She felt lightheaded. She could not believe this was happening. It was too much, to potent to absorb and to complex to digest all at once. She realized she was holding her breath. Belinda relaxed, exhaled and was very thankful to be leaning against a wall at that exact moment.

# Chapter Five

BELINDA AWOKE THE NEXT MORNING FEELING AS THOUGH the night before had been merely a dream. Could reality ever be so romantically transcendent? She took a deep breath and let it all come back. She recapitulated all the moments, allowed the memories to wash back over her.

The Fellow had invited them back to the club later that week, for a night of live jazz. She closed her eyes, breathed in deeply and tried to figure out what she was feeling. Excitement, intrigue, uncertainty and fear of the unknown; yes they were all there. When they'd all parted last night, she tried to keep her composure cool, detached, but she felt something beyond her control was happening.

His gaze was hypnotic, his smile knowing. She recalled the kiss goodnight on her cheek. His lips barely brushed against her skin; feathery, light, electric with the lingering promise of more. The memory made her stomach leap. It sent a delicious jolt throughout her being. The gleam in his eyes hinted that he also was very aware of something incendiary happening between them.

She was completely titillated by the possibilities here. And yet, even someone as well versed in Love's spiritual teachings as Belinda, she was still susceptible to the ego's pull, its tremendous hunger for dominance in all matters, especially those of the heart.

And so, the internal war for control over her emotions begun to wage. Questions, doubt and the utter uncertainty of it all aimed to trample all her excitement, elation and child-like wonder. She turned over, buried her face in the cool, soft down comfort of her pillow, hoping to banish the thoughts.

Belinda's spirit knew what she was failing to grasp in this tenuous moment was that Love's power, while intoxicating, flourished only in its elusiveness. Love thrived in the unknown, the unexplored. It was the ultimate realm of all possibility and creativity. As soon as you thought you had Love all figured out, that it was within your grasp, just like water it would slip through your fingers. Yet it was always laughing, teasing, forever playful, for Love always encouraged you to follow. Belinda knew all of this, but believing in the abstract notion was a far cry from experiencing and embracing the reality. Which right now was proving to be an altogether disconcerting matter.

And so, it was in those cracks, the crevices that doubt created, that the ego seeped in and took its sensuous hold. Insidiously, it methodically maneuvered to tip her off balance. Hence, it proved very difficult not to second-guess her initial feelings, especially when they occurred in such fragile dual parts of strangeness and exultant familiarity. But, Belinda had made a promise to Love. A promise to boldly go wherever Love led. She trusted, that as long as she stayed true to Love, she would not, could not, be lead astray. She sighed. It all sounded simple enough in theory.

But something about her chemistry with this Fellow made her feel as though something else was at work here, almost as if she was gently being led. That she had no choice but to follow. Should she just acquiesce? Trust in Love and ardently go wherever it led? She recalled the sage advice:

> *When one doesn't know what to do, don't do anything, take a deep breath.*
>
> *The answer will surely come.*

Belinda sat up, stretched her arms up over her head. She arched her back, relished the pleasant cracks going down her spine. Enough of this, she declared to herself, today there was more important matter's to be thinking about. Today would be a day of brilliant, prolific writing, she declared to the world. She slipped on a white, terry robe and padded to the lavatory and a shower. She smiled to herself, marveling, at how when you decided to live the life of your dreams, tremendous things truly were wont to happen from one moment to the next.

In the shower she tilted her head back, let the warm water envelope her nakedness, enfold her in its soothing caress. She suddenly felt an intrinsic sense of peace, safety, as though back in the fluid warmth of the womb. The feeling imparted an intuitive, primal sense of being taken care of by a larger entity, in this case a Mother, and that loving, knowing voice said,

*Trust. All would be well in the end.*

Belinda knew that living an inspired, creative and meaningful life really was a work of art in itself. Each breath was meant to be exalted, each moment filled with possibility and the sheer wonder of being alive. Oh, if only she could bottle such bliss, she yearned.

She was reminded of the words of artist Marcel Duchamp *"I like living, breathing better than working...my art is that of living. Each second, each breath is a work which is inscribed nowhere, which is neither visual nor cerebral, it's a sort of constant euphoria."*

Yes, she knew he was on to something: *a sort of constant euphoria.*

What a glorious notion indeed.

# Chapter Six

BELINDA FOUND IT VERY HARD TO CONCENTRATE THE NEXT few days. The unexpected situation of meeting this Fellow seemed to want to derail her from any productive creative efforts. Most certainly it dominated her thoughts, completely distracted her from her writing. Seeing him for the second time at the club's jazz night last evening only seemed to heighten her preoccupation and confusion.

Oddly they had hardly spoken throughout the evening. He was working, busy hosting an event in one of the private rooms. It was only just before the clock struck midnight and Belinda and her friends were preparing to leave that he appeared.

He had the uncanny ability to appear like an illusion, out of nowhere, with eyes flashing and be suddenly standing there right in front of her, solidifying before her eyes. Brilliant eyes fixed upon her, lips curled up in that knowing, little smile.

He proceeded to very succinctly ask Belinda for a date for the following evening. He must see her again, the sooner the better. Caught off guard, she hesitated for a moment. Her stomach had leaped, but in discomfort. It was happening much too fast. But in the next moment, she heard herself saying yes, that she would like that very much. A dinner date was confirmed.

And yet, having just awoken the next morning, with the bright light of a new day streaming through her bedroom window also came the startling light of reality and an onslaught of more dire uncertainty. She lay, eyes closed, focused on her breathing. She let herself detach from the emotions, float above the chaos. She was now witnessing everything from afar, above, as though she were a wise, old light-house trying to shed some much needed light and insight on the tumultuous waves that were coming in fast and furious, crashing on the rocks. Waves, like her ego that were trying to crush her excitement and resolve.

Belinda was very intrigued by this Fellow but there was still this puzzling feeling, a feeling she could not shake. It was hardly nefarious by any means, but it was different in a way that she could not articulate. It would undulate from jubilation to doubt to joy and back to doubt. The cycle was endless, the more she tried to analyze any of it, the stronger the feelings of doubt and anxiety became.

Suddenly, she was back on that emotional balance beam, teetering, fighting to keep her emotional and spiritual resolve. Her ego wanted her to tumble sideways into its abyss. If Belinda had been anyone else, those few cracks in her emotional fortitude would have been enough to tip her over but having nurtured a sense of spiritual tenacity for such a long time she was quickly able to reconnect with the only real thing in life; Love. She turned inward, invited truth into her awareness and guided herself back to her calm center and ultimately to balance.

There was absolutely no reason why she had to know what the meaning was of this encounter at this exact moment, she said to herself, even if the coincidences were dizzying and hypnotic. She would go with the flow, let it unfold, trust in the process and that the meaning would reveal itself soon enough. There was no rush.

How astoundingly powerful the ego was, she thought to herself. Why was it such an arduous task to just trust in Love and its process? Trust that a sense of mystery was a wonderful, profound and very necessary aspect not only in romance but in all of life as well. She knew this in her art but was hard pressed to apply it to romance.

Why was it so easy to scrutinize a moment to the point where it became so distorted from what was actually happening that it hardly resembled the unique and delightful truth any longer? Belinda was convinced that the constant analysis in life and in art was the work of your ego-need to control, most certainly it killed one's creativity, surely it would do the same for romance.

Belinda was reminded of the wise words of one of her favourite poets, John Keats, and a rebuttal to a critic attempting to analysis his art and his poetry. Keats said:

*"A poem needs understanding through the senses. The point of diving into a lake is not immediately to swim to the shore but to be in the lake, to luxuriate in the sensation of water. You do not work the lake out; it was an experience beyond thought. Poetry soothed and emboldened the soul to accept the mystery."*

He very well could be speaking of Love, for was budding Love not meant to be simply luxuriated in? Did Love not soothe and embolden the soul? Belinda knew she had to accept Love's intrinsic mystery, if she ever wanted to feel Love's truer, deeper nature and meaning. Inspired, she threw back the covers, headed to the kitchen to put on a pot of tea. She poked her head out the window. It was a clear, sunny day, the sky the most glorious shade of cerulean blue.

A brilliant day for a jaunt through Kensington Gardens, she decided. The thought pleased her immensely. After her ritualistic, leisurely tea, a read through of the Arts & Life section of the weekend edition of the Financial Times, she quickly showered. Her hair was still damp as she pulled it back into a braid. She slipped on a pair of tan corduroy trousers, donned an ivory cable knit sweater and her scuffed cognac-hued riding boots. On her way out, she grabbed her navy quilted jacket and a tweed newsboy cap and left the flat. Four seasons in one day, she smiled, God bless London weather.

———◆◆———

She entered the park at Albert Gate, headed toward West Carriage Drive. Eventually she arrived at the Italian Gardens, one of her favourite places in all of London, but today she was compelled to keep walking. She continued past the fountains, followed one of the footpaths that led toward the Round Pond. She breathed deeply, letting the fresh autumnal air fill and expand her lungs. The park was busy; tourists, families and numerous dog walkers all out reveling in the beauty of crispy leaves in vibrant shades of mustard yellow, candied orange and apple red.

She rounded the pond and set off on a path to the right that led back to the big Spire. Communing with nature always calmed, soothed her soul. She felt good, connected and knew it was the perfect moment to seek some inner guidance. After a few moments, she took a deep breath, closed her eyes and silently asked,

"Am I on the right path?"

Belinda opened her eyes. She remained tuned in to all her senses. She didn't see anything exceptional or interesting. Nor did she hear or smell anything out of the ordinary. She was waiting for a sign, or a coincidence that would be Love's answer, it was a creative leap in time and space, meant specifically for her.

"Excuse me, will you please tell me where we can find the Peter Pan statue?"

A woman had suddenly appeared and approached Belinda with the question.

"The Peter Pan statue is that way," she said and pointed

in the correct direction. "If you head back to the Italian Gardens, turn right and follow the path along Long Water, it will lead you right there". The woman thanked her and hurried away.

Well, Belinda mused, that was very interesting indeed. The reference to Peter Pan was most certainly pointing to something, a larger truth. She knew the workings of Love's signs were always subtle, the messages never got louder, only clearer. She thought about what Peter Pan symbolized. On the surface he represented eternal childhood, the boy who never wanted to grow up. But delving deeper one knew that childhood itself was the domain of eternal innocence, playfulness and a sense of wonder and timelessness.

Love itself was all of those elements. In our youth we were eternally carefree and optimistic about life. We were less jaded, less fearful, more adventurous and loved effortlessly, joyously, freely. We worried less and lived in the present constantly. Time had no bearing and truly did not exist when you were a child. We were too captivated by being constantly curious, constantly having fun in the present moment.

Belinda took the Peter Pan sign as a poignant message, an important reminder to "always keep the child in view" as Dickens so succinctly put it. To nurture and never lose sight of those very special child-like qualities in her own self. It was a brilliant sign indeed but still a little too nebulous for her liking. She hungered for further clarity.

At this point Belinda had returned to the Italian Gardens. She walked over to one of the benches on the eastern edge of the gardens, only a few paces away from the famous statue commemorating great physician Edward Jenner, and sat down. Looking out at the fountains Belinda sighed, how she adored those elaborate water gardens.

Prince Albert is said to have commissioned the

ornamental fountains and statues as a gift for his beloved wife, Queen Victoria, in the late 19<sup>th</sup> century. There were four larger fountains set in octagonal ponds around a more diminutive central fountain. At the north end there stood a grand structure with three large elegant archways that today mostly served as shelter for tourists visiting the gardens on rainy days. The outer edge of the fountains was dotted with massive stone urns and benches while the south end boasted an immense cement balustrade where water cascaded down a central sculpture of water nymphs into the Long Water, the body of water that separated Kensington Gardens from Hyde Park.

She never tired of the romantic mystique, the old-world allure of the Italian Gardens. She closed her eyes, breathed deeply, focusing her attention on her heart and decided to ask a more specific question, the one that had been nagging her since she had smelled his cologne that first night:

"Is this Fellow the man of my dreams?"

She slowly opened her eyes. The first thing she saw was a flashing amber light to her left. It sat on top of a park maintenance truck driving by across the way. She was compelled to follow the flashing amber light, mesmerized by it, until it started to pass the fountain to her right, then something else caught her eye. There, in the fountain pond, were two lovely swans paddling about. One was leading with its neck erect whilst the other followed, its neck gracefully arched. There were no other birds in the fountain.

Belinda's breath caught in her throat. She had wanted a clear sign and this was what she was given. It was too incredible. Didn't swans mate for life? She was positive they did. Her heart beat quickened. She blinked a few times to ensure she wasn't seeing an apparition. No, they were still there, graceful as ever.

Belinda was at a loss: could the Heavens really be telling

her something this profound? This soon? Was this truly a sign that this Fellow was her... She couldn't even finish the thought. Really? She took another deep breath. It was much too overwhelming a thought about someone she has just met.

She shook her head, looked at her watch and realized she only had a few hours to get a bunch of errands done before she had to get back to the flat to change for her date that evening. She would have to probe deeper into this sign another time.

As she walked away she could not help but hold the romantic vision of the two lovely swans in her mind. Yet, in her heart's eye, there was another image at the forefront: the flashing amber light. It had been the first sign. She saw it again, flashing, flashing. Caution, caution it seemed to say over and over. Well, at least it hadn't been a red light, she thinks, smiling ironically to herself.

Belinda pushed the image of the amber light out of her head preferring the spectacle of the two idyllic swans and sets off about her day. Alas, Belinda's spirit knew due to such insouciant abandon, she would have to learn one of Love's lessons the hard way.

# Chapter Seven

Belinda returned to the flat from her errands with only an hour to shower, dress and hop into a cab. They were to meet at a tapas restaurant on Marylebone High Street. She headed to the loo and quickly disrobed, dropping her clothes on top of the lavatory lid. In her haste she placed her watch on top of the pile. She did a quick double take; nervous with how precariously it lay perched on the pile of clothes.

The watch was a beloved birthday gift, designed in a classic men's style, with an oversized, round ivory face, big black roman numerals, framed in gold with a crocodile embossed tan leather strap that was worn to a fine patina from constant wear. Should it slip and fall, it would land directly on the hard tile floor. She then noticed the time on her watch and any concern for its fate was replaced with a sense of urgency to get ready and hopped in the shower.

Forty minutes later she was dressed and ready to go, having decided on a camel, V-neck cashmere sweater, a tailored herringbone blazer with brown patches at the elbows, slim navy trousers and navy, suede, moccasin-style loafers with little crests. Classic, elegant yet casual, said her reflection in the mirror. She reached for her Penhaligon's perfume bottle, applied the scent behind her ears, on her wrists. It was then that she realized something was missing.

Her watch. She walked over to the loo. There it was, on top of the pile of clothes, exactly where she'd left it.

She reached for it, but somehow it slipped through her fingers. She watched in horror and as if in slow motion as it fell flat face down on to the loo floor. She cringed at the loud clack sound of glass hitting the hard tile floor.

"Dammit," she muttered to herself

She knelt down, picked it up to assess the damage. She slowly turned it over and, thankfully, the face was not damaged. But, in the next instant, the most peculiar thing occurred. Belinda watched as several of the roman numerals cascaded to the bottom of the watch. The hair stood up on the back of her neck, it was the oddest thing to behold. Truly, it was as though time, literally, disintegrated right before her very eyes. She blinked, not really believing what she had just witnessed.

"How extraordinary," she murmured to herself

She gingerly placed the watch on her dresser. As she headed out the door she pondered the importance of timelessness. The fact that it seemed to be a recurring theme throughout the day was not lost on Belinda. First with the Peter Pan reference earlier that day in the park and now this. She knew time and it's passing really depended on your perception of it. How else could the day blow by at a manic pace for one, yet go excruciatingly slow for another? Ultimately, she felt it was a sign to remember to live in the present. To surrender to the here and now since it truly was ones only reality.

"Easier said then done," she thought to herself, "Especially when society lived and breathed by the clock".

She raised her arm to hail a black cab and was about to release the thought out of her head when a slight sense of foreboding crept into Belinda's heart. It told her she ought to seriously heed the day's messages, as everything happened for a reason and be it big or small it all was part of her life's natural rhythm and pointed to a larger picture that was unfolding. Pay attention, be patient, her heart seemed to say, or run the risk of the unknown repercussions.

———•◆•———

The date was going splendidly. Having been to the restaurant before, the Fellow expertly chose an array of succulent dishes. The place was busy; each table pullulated with chic, eager gourmands. Fire sizzled, steam rose from the open kitchen, the scent of fresh cilantro, lemon and grilled meats permeated the air. They sat, constantly smiling and chatting, across from each other. He was just as handsome as she remembered.

Oddest thing though, Belinda always seemed to forget how he actually looked when they were apart, only recalled the feelings and sensations he evoked within her. Seeing him in the flesh was like seeing him again for the first time and every time she was arrested by his striking, Byronic handsomeness.

Tonight he wore the same smart, black-rimmed spectacles, a snug aubergine colored cashmere jumper and a white patterned shirt underneath. The conversation flowed easily, rhythmically. They had so much in common, yet their respective life experiences were worlds apart. Underlying all of this, for Belinda, was the uncanny sense of familiarity. This excruciating detail truly bewildered her.

After dinner they walked about Marylebone High Street. Belinda linked her arm through his as he very proficiently explained the different types of architecture, which was a passion of his. At one point, he guided her over to a set of church steps, flanked with large stone balustrades on each side and pointed out the intricate details in the cornice above the heavy, wooden doorway.

He artfully maneuvered her so that she was on the step above him and it rendered them eye level. He continued to speak. His elocution was impeccable, melodious and trance-like. He then very gracefully and naturally turned her around to face him.

In that moment his scent wafted over her and the trance was broken. She was suddenly very awake. It's familiar bouquet of lavender and citrus, balmy spices, pine and hints of woody musk again evoked an unsettled feeling in her. She endeavored to push the feeling away and stared into his brilliant eyes and found herself saying

"I am quite fond of your cologne"

"Really? Are you sure? Perhaps you need a closer inspection darling" He said this with a mischievous grin and tilted his head to one side.

Belinda leaned in, traced the tip of her nose from the curve at the base of his neck up to his ear and breathed him in, deeply. He gently pulled her back, looked her in the eyes searchingly, and then slowly leaned in.

He first brushed his lips feather light against hers. The kiss then deepened, his tongue gently touched hers. Belinda felt an intense surge of electricity go through her at the connection. In the next moment they were kissing passionately. Their mouths seemed to meld, their breath filling each other's beings. Their lips moved silently, in perfect synchronicity, as though they had kissed a million times before. Belinda relaxed, melted into him as he clutched her closer.

She suddenly felt herself expand, leave her body and float up and away. Away from the two figures still locked in a fiery embrace. She felt herself spreading out, becoming boundless. She floated higher, further away. Away from Marylebone High Street, London, the sky and the world to a place of softness and light. She was bliss. She felt safe. She was everywhere and nowhere.

# Chapter Eight

THE NEXT DAY, AS BELINDA SAT AT HER LAPTOP ATTEMPTING to write at a café down the street, that kiss would flash into her head involuntarily. Each time it sent a delicious jolt directly to her loins. It was actually absurd how frequent and distracting it was. They had made plans to meet at the Italian Gardens in Kensington Park later that afternoon, her stipulation being only after she'd gotten a good amount of writing done.

Needless to say, it was hardly a productive day for her. The minutes, the hours do not move fast enough for one in this state, she mused. Then, finally it was time. Belinda arrived first. The park was quiet, the day brilliantly sunny and vast. Her love-glazed eyes saw the sky and park gardens an aquatint in Technicolor. The hues were vibrant, rich and dynamic as though Bonnard himself had painted the scene. Brush strokes of azure, lemon, violet, juniper and persimmon all swirled around her.

She swiftly made a beeline for the Italian Garden's fountains, as she secretly hoped to see her swans. No such luck. Darn, she was so sure they'd be there, if only to validate what she was feeling. Somewhat dejected, she turned around and walked back to the entrance on Bayswater Road near Lancaster Gate tube.

She saw his tall, lean frame approaching. Arms casually swinging, long legs striding toward her. He wore a gorgeous, long camel coloured cashmere coat, a pale pink shirt, dove-grey waistcoat and slim trousers with pin-cord stripes of washed out hues of white, pink, blue and yellow. She adored his bon-vivant style, how he always appeared to have dressed from the closet of Jay Gatsby or Sebastian Flyte.

As they came together, she smiled as he clutched her close, arching her backward as he swooped down and planted a long fervent kiss on her eager lips.

"Hello my darling girl. Don't you look enchanting..."

"Likewise, splendid trousers" she said.

"Thank you. Upon rising the sunlight wistfully reminded me of mornings in Capri, so I decided to dress for it." He said with a wink.

They continued walking on, hand in hand. He wanted to take her to a fun and kitschy café on Bayswater Road. The cafe paid a romantic homage to the ill-fated Princess Diana of Wales. Hundred's of pictures of her blonde loveliness and doleful blue eyes were scattered all over the walls, covering every available inch of wall space.

They ordered two lattes and sat outside on the front terrace. They sat close, like all new lovers, their hands or knees always wanting, needing to touch. At one point, he really opened up to Belinda about his past, the intimate details of his life. It was a tale that undulated, full of family sensitivities, challenges, pain and loss but also much beauty, excitement and creativity.

At the end of it Belinda felt she had been privy to another dimension to this Fellow, a softer more vulnerable side. A side that was very deftly masked by the extremely self-assured and cultivated veneer he projected. She felt a rush of affection and compassion for him. In that moment, something deep in her heart, something intuitive told her that regardless of what happened they had been destined to meet. Destined to share, to touch, to Love and ultimately to heal. She leaned over, gave him a soft kiss and looking him in the eyes said,

"Thank you for sharing so much of yourself with me. I want you to know I think you're wonderful just for being you."

He smiled back, then took her face in his hands and kissed her deeply

"That is the kindest thing anyone has ever said to me," he said gently.

He then winked and stood, said he would go in to pay for their coffees.

Belinda took the moment to enjoy the waterfall of warmth that flooded over her. Alas, she was still undecided as to how she truly felt about him. She found him extremely attractive, utterly dashing and beyond intriguing. His old-world comportment, British accent, eccentric style and air of savoir-faire truly made him a modern day Renaissance man in Belinda's eyes. The combination was quite heady and she knew she could not have invoked a more romantic and beguiling hero to be courting her in London. Truly, she felt as though she were living her very own London fairy-tale. But, whilst she enjoyed the sense of propinquity when being with him she still needed more time to figure out exactly where her heart stood in all of this.

That moment evoked such a wild, familiar happiness within her that it reminded her of a passage about real, true Love from one of her favourite novels, *The Pursuit of Love*, by Nancy Mitford:

*"...It is described as seeing someone in the street who you think is a friend, you whistle and wave and run after him, and it is not only not the friend, but not even very like him. A few minutes later the real friend appears in view, and then you can't imagine how you ever mistook that other person for him."*

Was this Fellow indeed her Beloved? Her *authentic face of Love*? She needed a sign, a clear sign. She would even take a clue pointing in the right direction right now, something that would reveal the true meaning of his presence in her life.

He returned and they were about to walk off when Belinda, holding her purse in her hands, realized she hadn't properly looped the clasp and fumbled to do so. Abruptly, something fell out of her purse. It landed on the pavement at her feet with an odd clunk. The Fellow quickly, and very gallantly, knelt down to pick it up for her.

When Belinda realized what it was, she stopped. It was her silver *I love you* stone. Belinda's heart began to pound. Was this really happening right now, she thought to herself? He looked at the stone, curiously turned it over. Reading what it said, he then looked Belinda directly in the eyes and then pressed the stone into the palm of her hand. Belinda felt her face go bright scarlet. How the devil did that happen? What was going on? She was mortified and amazed at the same time.

She met his brilliant gaze, their eyes locked, time stopped. The world seemed to fall away around them and enveloped in a kaleidoscope of hues their forms were transported to eternity and beyond. In the next moment they were back on Bayswater Road, the dreary grey asphalt with all the cacophony of city traffic engulfing them. The magic had passed. She quickly composed herself, and softly said thank you.

She was barely able to tear her eyes away from his; why did she feel as though he could read what was going on in her head? She put the stone back into her purse and slipped the strap onto her shoulder. They carried on. The Fellow started to recount a story but Belinda was only half listening. She was trying to process the meaning of what had just transpired.

She had carried that stone around for the better part of a year and half and it had never fallen out of her purse before, never mind having it handed back to her by a man she was having such complex feelings about. What did it mean? Not to mention moments before she had asked Love for a sign, a clue as to why he was in her life? Was this her sign? Was her *I love you* stone telling her that he was indeed someone worth loving?

She knew she already felt a deep affection for him and more importantly that she enjoyed the scent of his *essence* - that wonderful, very special, very unique and primordial scent that was to be found in a Lover's ear. Since she could remember Belinda had intuitively taken to knowing that if she enjoyed the scent in her Beloved's ear she knew they were off to a very propitious beginning. That being said, she was still uncertain about how she truly felt about this Fellow, the feelings he evoked within her were so unlike anything else she'd ever experienced.

And yet, she also knew that Love, when it came, would not necessarily come in a rush of clear, profound emotion or in a package that she'd even recognize. She knew she had to remain open and ultimately trust her heart to guide her and in time certainty would follow. Trouble was, she didn't realize what a feat it would be to do just that. Especially considering how quickly things were moving and how often she was assailed with such conflicting emotions.

# Chapter Nine

THE NEXT MORNING BELINDA WAS SEATED AT HER KITCHEN table trying, quite unsuccessfully, to read through the weekend newspaper. Alas, having read the same sentence for the third time she finally gave up. Irritated, she put down her cup of tea and pushed away her barely eaten almond croissant.

Typically, a steaming cup of English Breakfast Tea, served in a lovely porcelain cup and saucer, a fresh almond croissant from the local patisserie and the Arts & Life section of the weekend Financial Times was something she relished each Saturday morning. Not today. Today she somehow could not muster up an ounce of the usual delight she took from this little weekend ritual.

Whilst her spirit yearned to relish in the fact that it was a new, glorious day where anything could happen, her mind was adamant on analyzing the past, worrying about the future and fretting how things were progressing in London. How did she feel about it all? She stared out the kitchen window onto Pimlico Road and let her mind succumb to contemplation.

A very inspired, yet also unknown pull had compelled her to come to London. She knew when she set off on this journey it was unchartered territory, a romantic adventure. When she arrived she had a clear and important focus, her writing and the intention to luxuriate in each and every moment of this magical and meditative journey. So, what had happened? She'd started out on course but somehow along the way she'd allowed the superlative joy she found in just waking up in London and her writing to become superseded by the complete and utter distraction of this newfound romance.

And yet today, to be quite frank, she was absolutely bored with it. Completely and utterly bored. Bored with the tedious, endless preoccupation of it all. Bored with how it dictated the sweep and swell of her emotions. Bored also with all the seemingly wild coincidences associated with it. Bored with the fact that she hadn't been able to concentrate on her writing. Bored with all the noxious analyzing. Surely, if she didn't curtail all of it soon she'd drive herself utterly mad.

Instead of being calm, trusting and present she found herself oscillating between the past and the future, constantly fraught with uncertainty and anxiety over every coincidence, invariably questioning their meaning and wondering if she was on the right path. When had she turned into such a soppy mess? Where had the woman of conviction she knew herself to be disappeared to? She had to stop this madness. She needed to meditate. Meditation and turning inward to the truth always brought her back to Love and her peaceful center.

---

An hour later she was feeling much more civilized. Focused and centered she set off to a café off of South Molten Street near Bond Street to produce an abundance of writing.

Belinda noted again the amount of sheer and utter contented bliss and connectedness she experienced whilst she was writing. How absolutely peaceful, comforting and expansive she found the process and the experience. Whilst writing nothing was complicated, she even relished the uncertainty, trusting it to bring forth the desired creative response or inspiration she needed. There was no anxiety; she intuitively trusted the process and her conviction in that process and her creative spirit and its guidance never failed her in her experience. It always felt supremely *right*. Time dissolved and the day resplendently and productively evaporated.

She also exulted in the sense of freedom and independence associated with her writing. It had nothing to do with another person or thing. She also need not rely on anyone else to connect to the divine source or to execute it. Unlike a job where you had to be hired and then could be made redundant, her writing granted her an all-encompassing power to create at her will. It had become integral as the blood coursing through her veins, as necessary as breathing. It was her private outlet of creative expression and expansion. Her unique way of expressing her inner light to the world that no one could take away from her.

Her afflatus was her spirit and its vehicle was her conscious mind. When these two were in harmony there was an alertness, an aliveness in her own being that flowed in perfect synchronicity with life and thoughts and ideas easily flowed and manifested into words on a page. Thus with this result it was literally as though her spirit's intent, Love's universal intent, was realized every time.

Yet, Belinda hesitated to stake a claim to it. Intuitively she knew that she was a mere conduit for which a larger entity was at work. Many a time this creative expression that manifested itself into writing seemed to just be using her, lovingly, as any artist uses an instrument to create its desired work of art. It was a release of one's conscious light with the ultimate hope of inspiring and igniting the world with it.

It truly was a magnificent feeling. Yet, why was it so bloody difficult to apply these insights to romance as well?

Romantic love was surely just as creative an expression as her art. Yes, perhaps that was the answer. She felt she had stumbled onto something quite important. Trust the romantic process, honour the dating stages and rituals, as there was wisdom in taking the time to allow things and people to unfold themselves organically to each other so that romantic Love too would then be able to flourish and bring on a perfectly blended cornucopia of emotions, feelings and outcomes. If only, she sighed. Alas, it was also Belinda's secret hope, her heart's desire that by writing about what was happening to her she would also glean a few personal insights along the way.

———•◆•———

One week later the sky was overcast, a brooding and uncertain shade, neither white nor grey but rather patches of light and dark like partially sullied virgin wool that had been pulled across the sky.

Belinda was headed to catch the tube. She had been invited over to the Fellow's flat for luncheon. She was looking forward to it but was also apprehensive without knowing exactly why. As she took a seat on the tube she pondered the fact that they had only known each other for a few short weeks, yet that familiar kinship feeling whenever she was around him only continued to grow.

This fact also seemed to assuage some of her uncertainty, if only fleetingly. This familiarity had now taken on an almost otherworldly quality, like she'd always known him or perhaps knew him in another time or life. But what did it mean for this life pray tell? She stood. Her stop had arrived.

He lived in red brick, low-rise multi-flat, on a leafy street in Belsize Park. An area that she did not know very well but instantly loved its quaintness and walking proximity to the

Heath. He buzzed her up, had the door swung open before she could even knock. He quickly gathered her up in his arms, sending a trail of kisses down her neck. He ushered her in, insisted that she take a seat, just relax.

"I have everything prepared, you just amuse yourself in the sitting room for a few minutes darling girl" and disappeared down the hall.

The sound of crockery, preparation, clattered down the hall. Belinda took the opportunity to meander about. Unsupervised she was able to freely poke, lift, sift and glance at whatever piqued her interest. It was a superbly decorated flat. The space was bright, airy and whilst the walls were painted white the sitting room was filled with many dark, earthy, exquisite bibelots he'd obviously hand selected with the utmost care on his various travels from all over the world.

Literally, wherever the eye landed there was an exquisite antique, hint of his childhood or curiosity that beckoned to be caressed or inquired about. The scent in his flat also evoked the feeling of another time and place. It was leathery, musky with the hint of amber and the exotic and hinted at a man with voluptuary tastes.

Belinda picked up a small pile of old, yellowed letters, bundled together with a piece of twine. She pulled one out enough to only read to whom it was addressed. It was a handwritten letter, in a child's slanting scrawl, written to Buckingham Palace. Belinda recalled the story he had told her, how as a child he had sent numerous letters requesting formal visits to the palace as a future pupil of interior architecture and design. How utterly bold and precocious he must have been as a young boy. There was also the complete collection of Shakespeare's plays, a multitude of art and architecture books. Moroccan ashtrays and decorative dishes dotted various surfaces.

Belinda wandered over to his desk for a gander. There were many various postcards; one in particular seemed to dominate. It was of a strikingly beautiful African-tribal boy in full headdress, his face and body covered in ceremonial scars. It reminded Belinda of the realities of being born into a life lived by nature's primal laws. It seemed out of place amongst the profusion of material beauty he surrounded himself with, yet it was also quite fitting of man who had as many interests and dimensions as she suspected he did.

Her glance then fell to the chestnut leather desk blotter where gorgeous vanilla stationary paper, sleek pens, a magnifying glass and matching letter opener both with bejeweled handles lay in perfect order. She spotted a half written note, his penmanship was exquisite, and her curiosity prevailed. She began to read the note but suddenly felt the hair on the back of neck stand up. She was being watched. She whirled around. He stood in the room, brilliant eyes flashing, looking quite bemused and holding two plates of quiche and heaps of rocket salad. How long had he been standing there?

"Luncheon is served darling..." punctuating his comment with a mischievous wink.

---

Afterwards they settled down to some show and tell. He put on some music and pulled out numerous family photos, including pictures of himself as a child with his family. He was a brilliant storyteller; enchantingly recounted the narrative of his life, the tales behind many of the beautiful objects around them. He had travelled and worked extensively all over the world. Belinda found it all entrancing.

At one point, as they were going through a collection of

postcards he had collected over the years, one in particular caught her eye. As soon as she saw it Belinda's heart skipped a beat.

"Wait, may I please see the one you just passed? Were those swans?"

He handed her the postcard. It was indeed of two swans swimming in very familiar looking surroundings. The back of the postcard revealed they were, in fact, swimming in Hyde Park. Belinda could hardly believe her eyes. The swans were in the exact formation as the ones she herself had seen in the Italian Gardens fountains weeks ago after she had asked Love if this Fellow was her soulmate. Her breath caught in her throat. Here, in her hand, she held an exact replica of that image: one swan with a straight neck led the other with its neck arched.

"Pray tell, what's so special about that one darling?"

"How odd… I just saw this exact image at the Italian Garden's a little while ago. It's uncanny that you have a postcard with the exact image… " She handed him back the postcard and started to leaf through the rest, endeavoring to change the subject.

A little while later still somewhat unsettled Belinda made a hasty excuse to get going. He walked her to the door and gallantly held out her coat for her. Belinda, still preoccupied with the swan's postcard, absently thanked him as she slipped her arms into her jacket. He opened the door and she was about to walk out when he gently pulled her back from the doorway.

"Hey, there… aren't you forgetting something gorgeous girl?"

He placed his hand on the small of her back and, like an expert dance partner, arched her body into to his and kissed her deeply. Alas, this time, not even his deliciously sensual overtures were able to sway her from her preoccupations.

Back at the flat, Belinda was seated in the dark on the sofa. The window was shut and the room was in complete silence except for the intermittent tap of the tree branches on the window. She still wore her jacket and shoes. The clock on the mantle suddenly chimed the hour and she was transported back to the day she first saw the swans.

She had been seated on a bench in front of the fountains in the Italian Gardens, having just met the Fellow, fraught with juxtaposing emotions and seeking a sign. She wanted a sign that confirmed if indeed this Fellow was her soul mate. She opened her eyes and again saw the two swans in her mind's eye. She recalled how amazed she was at such a romantic symbol. And yet, she seemed to also recall there was something she was forgetting, something else she saw that day that was equally as important. But for some odd reason it eluded her in that moment.

Her mind flashed back to the postcard, the staggering coincidence of his having one of such a similar image was highly improbable. What was the message for her? That she was on the right path, seemed sure, but what else did it mean? Could it be that they were actually... Dare she say it? She took a deep breath and allowed herself to actually indulge the thought.

"Was this a sign that she'd met her soulmate?"

Her mind reeled at the possibility. She barely knew him for goodness sake. And yet, there was that deep, unmistakable feeling of familiarity, as if their spirits acknowledged each other whenever they were together. It had been there the moment their eyes met, that first night at the restaurant. Whenever she was around him, she felt such a deep sense of connection to him. Were these the burgeoning feelings of true and eternal love? Yet if so, why did they come with equal amounts of uncertainty and discomfort?

# Chapter Ten

OSTENSIBLY CRAVING SOME CREATIVE INSPIRATION, WHEN IN reality all she was really looking for was a distraction, had Belinda en-route to the Romantics Exhibit at the Tate Britain. It had become a weekly routine to prioritize these creative jaunts be it an exhibit at a gallery or museum, an interesting talk or film, opera or play. She found these expeditions gloriously uplifting and inspiring for her spirit, a true creative necessity. Today walking through the exhibit at the Tate Britain she hoped to lose herself in the quixotic images of romantic period works by masters such as Henry Fuseli, JMW Turner, John Constable and Samuel Palmer.

She desperately needed to get back on track, the past few days had been ridiculously unproductive in terms of her writing. And, having analyzed her feelings in regards to the Fellow to the point of distraction, she decided she needed to simply abandon this ceaseless emotional tug of war if only for her creativity's sake. She was in London, living out a heroic, creative dream, writing her first book and being romanced by a fascinating man. So what if things were moving a little too fast for her liking? Wasn't that just a reflection of how simpatico they actually were?

Belinda had always been quite prudent in previous romances, setting the pace and never jumping in to intimacy too quickly. But things were different with this Fellow. They seemed to be at exactly the same place in their lives. He was just as ready, open to Love and spoke candidly and easily about marriage and wanted a family of his own.

And yet, Belinda could not deny the nagging feeling that something wasn't sitting right with her. He seemed so sure though, she valiantly tried to take comfort in his certainty.

But alas, lately she was also being visually assailed with cautionary signs. That pesky amber light, the elusive image that had appeared before she had seen the swans, had become ubiquitous. She tried to avoid it but it was relentless in catching her eye, from crosswalks to black cab stations to construction zones.

Caution, caution, caution was its constant cry. She found herself repeatedly having to push its menacing reminder away.

"What's there to fret about?" she asked herself. This romance was unfolding like the perfect dream. Was it so important that her writing had fallen to the wayside? Love and romance were supposed to trump everything. Weren't they? Even though her time in London would come to an end soon enough and she would be faced with some harsh realities, for the moment she just wanted to relish the delicious feeling of falling in Love. Surely she was allowed that, no? So, relish it she did.

# Chapter Eleven

A FEW WEEKS LATER BELINDA WAS INVITED TO SEE LA BOHÈME at The English National Opera with her best London chum. It was an opera she had long wanted to see, a superlative Love story, albeit a tragic one. As she dressed, deciding on an ivory tuxedo suit, black silk blouse with a high collar and voluminous sleeves, she could not help but feel somewhat unsettled at how Mimi, the heroine in La Bohème, met with such a lamentable demise in the end.

Was her destined attendance at this particular opera and her mixed feelings about the Fellow perhaps trying to tell her something about her own current lover's dalliance? Was there perhaps an equally heartbreaking, although hopefully not as fatal, demise in store for her and this romance? She shook her head and laughed, chided herself for being so overly dramatic. She checked herself in the hallway mirror, dabbed a bit of rouge on her cheeks and promptly pushed the thoughts away, choosing to focus on the building excitement of the night ahead and left the flat.

Afterward, still dizzy from the intense emotions the opera evoked within her, Belinda met up with the Fellow for a nightcap. The combination of a full moon, a mesmerizing operatic romance and her own current Love story in full swing had Belinda's heart singing and placed her in a very amorous mood that evening.

They ended up at the Fellow's flat, lying intertwined on his sofa, chatting over a glass of red wine by candlelight. She still wore her evening clothes, minus her tuxedo jacket, which lay draped over a chair. He was in a faded V-neck t-shirt and pajama bottoms, amusingly juxtaposing Belinda's fancy attire. He lay on his back, she on her side, perfectly tucked under his arm with her head on his chest.

Belinda lazily listened as he told her about his day. She was not sure what was making her more intoxicated, the wine or the musky scent of his male skin through his t-shirt combined with the dulcet tone of his voice. His voice was so deep, melodious, transfixing; she could listen to him just speak for hours.

Coming back from her reverie she suddenly realized he had stopped talking. Belinda lifted her head, assumed he may have dosed off but he was awake. He met her gaze, looked at her face with sensuous, half-closed eyes.

"I'd like to tell you something" he said and continued " I was telling a mate at work about you today and he asked me what about you made you so special to me. I told him it was quite simple."

He paused here for a moment, looked searchingly into her eyes. She met his gaze, tilted her head to one side and smiled encouragingly. He continued and whilst he spoke he traced her cheekbone and lips with his finger.

"It's very simple, I told him, she's not the girl I've always been waiting for but rather the girl I've always wanted to meet..." He pauses here again and asked, "Do you understand the difference darling?"

Belinda, completely overcome with emotion, could only nod. She was utterly transfixed by those brilliant eyes. He kissed her then, deeply, as if to punctuate the intensity of his emotions. Then in one sweeping motion he got up, gathered her into his arms and carried her to the bedroom.

They came together hurriedly, purposefully, their bodies arching towards each other in mutual need and desire. They could not remove each other's clothes fast enough. His hands explored the contours of her body with sensual artistry and intensity. He pushed her down onto the bed. Belinda leaned her head back, closed her eyes in anticipation. He lay on top of her, kissed her neck and grasped her breast as she arched her back in complete surrender. She was his instrument; ready to be played pianissimo style, slowly building to that rapturous crescendo. No, she was a long supple cast of clay, ready to be stretched and molded and he her brooding, brilliant artist, lovingly, sumptuously sculpting his masterpiece.

Eyes locked they reached ecstatic heights over and over, only to fall back to earth drenched, exhausted. Belinda, her body still rocking with pleasure, knew she was precisely where she was meant to be in that exact moment in time.

———◆———

A short time later, he rose to fix them a drink. Belinda, still lying down, raised her arms above her head. She languidly stretched out, relished the feeling in her Love-weary muscles. She sat up, gathered the wrinkled white sheets to her bare breasts, when suddenly she noticed something glinting in the moonlight on the bed beside her. She reached for it and as she picked up the object, she let out a gasp.

It was her necklace with the soulmate charm. The necklace she had sworn she would not remove until she met the man of her dreams. She had even told the Fellow of this vow and its importance since he had queried her on the unusual charm and its significance.

It must have come off whilst they were making-love…

How could that be? Her necklace had never come off before. Belinda's mind reeled. The room started to expand. Completely dazed, she lifted the necklace to show him what had happened when he came back into the bedroom. He carried two low-ball glasses and was swirling the amber coloured liquid around. She heard her heart beat in her ears, the sound of ice-cubes clinking against the glass was in the distance, muffled, faraway.

"Look" she said, not recognizing her own voice.

She was not looking at him but rather at her necklace in her raised hand.

"My necklace must have come off..."

Belinda, too caught up in the moment, its meaning and its magnitude, did not hear his response.

# Chapter Twelve

THE FEW WEEKS THAT FOLLOWED WERE COMPLETE, UTTER bliss. Passionate beyond measure, a romantic whirlwind with no end in sight, or so it seemed. Strangely, during much of it, Belinda had the oddest sensation of being detached from it all. She was outside of herself, not actually participating but observing, witnessing the romantic melee unfold.

The feeling was much like a bystander safely watching from the sideline as a tumultuous, run-away roller coaster thundered by. All of it was indeed brilliant fodder for her creativity and book and she did, truthfully, endeavor to write most days but ended up too preoccupied. This strange prescience within her continued for a while, intuitively it cautioned it was building, culminating to something.

Nevertheless, each day Belinda watched herself, a silent witness to her own life, as she recklessly went about each day not heeding the signs or the discomfort in her own heart but convinced herself that everything was exactly as she had wanted it to be. Alas, as Belinda's spirit knew, laws of the universe always prevailed and what one resisted only persisted. And suddenly, predictably, it all went sideways.

A few days later, they were seated at a café in Covent Garden, having met for a quick coffee before the Fellow headed to work, and Belinda to a valiant attempt at writing.

The coffee house walls were painted a chalky black, crystal chandeliers dripped overhead and the sweet aroma of steamed milk and ground coffee beans tinged the air.

They sat at a table by the large front window. Belinda noticed the pane was covered in condensation; the water ran down the window in tear-like streaks. She turned her back to the unsettling image and mustered up a cheerful smile for the Fellow. The conversation started out pleasantly enough but somehow, somewhere along the way it took a very curious and frightful turn. Unyieldingly, reality reared its pernicious head yet again and Belinda was forced to confront what she had intentionally put off since they had met.

As he spoke, the Fellow's endlessly beguiling British accent took on a firm, almost menacing tone as he began to voice his many misgivings about the reality of their situation. Since she was due to leave soon, what did this mean for them? What was her plan? What did she want? Could she see herself in London? Had she given thought to any of this? Why had she not communicated any of it to him? As he spoke his voice began to escalate, Belinda shifted uncomfortably in her seat.

She said, rather quietly, that she had just been enjoying the feeling of falling in Love. Surely, she was allowed that, and beamed him a wide smile. Her attempt at levity was unable to penetrate the thick cloud of gravitas rapidly swirling around him. Those brilliant eyes suddenly took on a very piercing look; his expression grew dark and quite earnest.

He continued on as if Belinda had not said a word. Things have moved much too fast, he declared superciliously. Perhaps it was best to take a break. Some distance would give them the perspective to properly access their situation. Did Belinda even want to truly settle in London? What about a visa? What about work? Writing a book surely wouldn't pay the bills. And pray-tell, when she did return to Canada how were they supposed to continue to get to know one another if they had a whole ocean between them?

She started to protest his iniquitous calculations but not being exactly sure about where she stood and what she exactly wanted, she caught herself. It was clear he'd thought a lot about all of this. Belinda, on the other hand, had clearly not. She did say she knew she would like for them to continue getting to know each other. Why couldn't they just let it continue as is, let things unfold naturally, organically?

Overly romantic and completely naïve, was his riposte. The fact that she would have such jejune notions about something so serious only seemed to frustrate and irritate him further and he waved off any further rebuttals without consideration. He felt if this relationship was to work, Belinda needed to reflect on what she truly wanted for herself, and if that involved a life in London, beyond him.

It was very apparent he had made up his mind. And, that his way was the ideal way to handle the situation; for the both of them. Clearly, there did not appear to be any room for discussion. He suddenly looked at his watch, then stood and gathered his cap and coat. Belinda sat there and watched him, from a detached emotional distance. She was calm, acutely present. She could hear the soothing sound of her heart beating. He then leaned over and briskly kissed her on the lips saying, they'd chat more in few days. That, perhaps, some distance would give them both some desired perspective, and with that comment bounded out the door.

Belinda calmly got up and walked out of the café. The clamour on the street jarred her back to what had just happened and the fearful and tearful repercussions set in. How quickly you were ripped from that quiet, safe, inner sanctum, only to be left feeling alone and exposed to life's illusions. And yet if she truly believed only Love was real, what was actually happening inside her right now?

"Was this pain real?" she tearfully questioned herself. "Or was it rather her thoughts about her unconscious actions and her ego's need for blame and dominance in all matters that were actually the cause of her pain?"

Quite frankly Belinda didn't care in that moment, she felt completely gutted, left in an obfuscated state. Had that conversation actually just happened? Surely her heart would say that it had. She felt as though her poor heart had been torn from her chest, violently shaken, reprimanded only to be left sobbing on the cold hard floor. And yet, somehow and quite grudgingly, she could see his beastly point.

Belinda had been remiss in not thinking about anything beyond enjoying the moment. If she was honest with herself, she knew she was also not thinking, rather not paying attention to other things, important things, signs and whisperings from her heart. But really, did he have to be so cold and malevolent about it all? It was a lot to swallow in one sitting and while she may have appreciated a little more tenderness and compassion in his tone, his queries did beg for an answer.

———◆———

The days that followed had Belinda doing some purposeful reflection. Seated by her sitting-room window, wrapped in a wooly tartan throw with a cup of tea she contemplated, meditated, asked Love for divine inspiration and guidance as to what she should be doing.

Was she on the correct path? Or were these feelings of unease telling her she had indeed strayed off? Was she just frightened of making the wrong decision? What did she want? Did she want to live permanently in London?

She knew she adored the city and had always felt a very natural affinity with it but picking up and moving to another country was a far bigger order then deciding to take a romantic adventure abroad.

When she'd set out on this contemplative journey it was with the sole conviction of connecting with her creative spirit, to try and satiate her spirit's seemingly unquenchable thirst for truth, meaning and creativity. To ultimately live the life of her dreams and she trusted the rest would figure itself out. And by rest, she meant romantic Love.

She had come seeking inspiration for her writing and life. Seeking creativity and beauty in every work of art, sunset and waking moment. Seeking authenticity and truth in each experience, encounter and trusted that her path would, at some point in the divine timing of things, also coincide with that great romantic Love she was also seeking and knew was seeking her. Belinda paused as a revelation suddenly struck her.

All this seeking, it seemed to contradict so many things, especially her trust in divine guidance and timing. Perhaps, she wondered, it was not her purpose to "seek" at all. Perhaps, those wonderful and ephemeral things in life are not to be sought. For how could you truly be present, enjoy the beauty and bounty available in the present if your attention was constantly focused on what you were supposedly searching for? Surely looking so hard could easily cause you to miss what was right in front of you. Perhaps our purpose was meant to just *be*. Be in the present moment. Be present with the people we Love. Be still. Be grateful. Just *be one* with life as is and thus connect with the glory of just *being alive*. She knew all this on many intuitive levels but why was it so difficult to put it into practice in everyday life?

What if she gave up all the seeking, she wondered, and

was patient, listened, followed the natural rhythm of her life and just trusted the process more? The mere notion sent her ego into a tailspin for its death was found in the present. And yet, if a tiny, humble acorn had all the intelligence it needed within to turn into a glorious, massive, wise oak tree surely we humans had also been given our own brand of intelligence at birth that was built into our DNA to help us traverse this path we called life and realize our full potential?

Yes, all you had to do was look to nature for so many answers *"Look at the lilies, they neither toil nor spin"*, went the age-old biblical proverb. They simply and gracefully trusted the process of life, stayed true to their unique unfolding. They knew that they would be cared and provided for – and they were.

Truly, all of life's abundance was available for our sharing. It was here, in that still quiet place in your heart, waiting to be delivered, unfolded at your very feet, if you truly believed and were still enough to see and feel it was so. Do not all of life's most exhilarating moments and passionate feelings literally "come to you"? More so than not, brilliant ideas, inspired thoughts or rushes of emotions came from *within*, not from out there.

Magnificent notions, esteemed revelations, all of them bubble forth from within, from the depths of your very own soul. Truly, it was one's own endless, creative fountainhead within. Yes, she knew she was on to something. That these revelations must be pointing to a pansophic truth. She endeavored to tap into that stillness, that trust in the flow and abundance of life. Just *BE* with her spirit. Usually it came quite easily but lately connecting to that inner voice too had become illusive, even fickle. Belinda recalled from ancient wisdom teachings that life was a mirror and that if it appeared illusive and fickle it was reflecting back her very own fickle and illusive state of mind.

Problem was, she had not anticipated things getting so complicated. It was as though Love's flow had somehow brutally, heartlessly hit a brick wall. She knew the blocks were within. She hadn't known what the future would hold but going into the unknown was what she had sought, no? But now, having met someone on this journey, it was interesting how this new and unexpected dynamic made her question her original motives.

Should she alter her path for Love? Or, should Love coincide perfectly with her path? Did it ever fit together so neatly? How far off her path was too far, even for Love? She knew she had a deep affection for this Fellow and would happily continue getting to know him; but to talk about moving continents was premature even for one as dedicated to Love as Belinda. She decided to put the quandary into abeyance for now and allow the emotions to digest for a while.

Belinda spent the next few days focused on her writing, she found it cathartic, comforting. She also took long meditative rambles in her beloved Kensington Gardens and walked along London's cobblestone streets, immersing herself in the city that she adored with eyes anew. Could she picture herself actually living here? Alas, it was hardly a feat for her to imagine.

For Belinda, London was very much like an old and sentimental Lover; all at once familiar, filled with fond, sensual memories, one that also knew precisely and exquisitely which heartstrings to stroke in order to get the desired effect from her.

Belinda and the Fellow had sporadic communication over the next week and whilst Belinda felt that this new development was a positive and evolutionary step in their getting to know one another, he seemed resolute in his decision that the best thing for the both of them right now was to go their separate ways. At least till life put them both in the "right" place.

Belinda did not understand why he felt the need to be so capricious. Nor did she agree with how morbidly he was painting the entire situation. Surely, they didn't have to chuck everything? Why throw out the baby with the bathwater? Wasn't there a middle ground? Apparently not. Their phone conversation ended with the mutual decision to move forward as friends. It was also decided that in the mean time it would be best to take a break from any contact or communication. For perspective and some heartfelt reflection.

Belinda rang off completely stupefied. Had that conversation actually occurred? Really? How could such a wondrous and seemingly inviolable romance fizzle down to this? It was all too banal, too mundane an ending for a courtship that had the makings of a grand and truly epic Love story. What about all those glorious signs? The swans, the love stone moment and then her soulmate necklace divinely coming off the first time they made love. Could she have misread those signs that appallingly? Alas, what a pity that would be.

Belinda spun around the sitting room looking for something to hurl at the wall, she wanted to break something, to destroy something. To release this pent up tension and frustration with herself and her utterly unconscious actions. When suddenly, there came a completely unexpected and peculiar emotion. It pierced through the blinding anger, gloom and seemingly bottomless pit of heartache and arrived with a very subtle but also very real dose of ... Relief. With it came warm and comforting tidings. She exhaled, sank into the nearest chair, allowed the relaxing, liquid warmth permeate her heart, limbs, fingertips and toes. Sweet relief, that some hugely erroneous experience had been averted. Her heart knew that with it a very difficult evolutionary lesson had lovingly, peacefully been by-passed for her.

# Chapter Thirteen

THE WAVES OF NAUSEA BEGAN TWO AND HALF WEEKS AFTER that conversation. The first time Belinda noticed it she attributed it to something she may have eaten. The second time she figured it was because she had skipped lunch whilst caught up with writing. The third time was when she started to worry.

She could seldom recall experiencing such perpetual bouts of nausea before. She pushed it out of her mind and took extra care in what and when she ate. Then came the sudden fatigue. She was exhausted by 8pm most evenings and found she had to take naps in the afternoon. It was only when these symptoms did not abate that Belinda knew she had to confront what she had suspected from day one.

She walked into her sitting room, grabbed her purse off the armchair and sat down on the sofa. She took a deep breath and begun to rifle through her purse looking for her diary. She was very meticulous in tracking these things. And so, there it was, in black in white. According to the dates, her cycle and when they had last made love, she very well could be pregnant.

"Brilliant," she said sarcastically to herself.

Belinda leaned back as she allowed this thought to sink in. She'd never been in this predicament before. She adored children and knew in her heart that she wanted to have a child, one day, but it had always included being married to the man of her dreams as the Father. Not ever, in her wildest nightmares, did she imagine she may be bringing a baby in to this world; alone, in a foreign land and somewhat estranged from the baby's Father.

In all honesty, if she looked at the actual timeline of their romance some would say she barely knew the Fellow. The entirety of their magical courtship had merely been a few months. All that passion and promise only to result in such a quick demise made Belinda's stomach knot and eyes well up.

Could this truly be happening to her? Really? Spiritually, she felt every child conceived and brought into this world was a blessing. That being said if this truly was her destiny then so be it. There were still a few more weeks before she knew for sure. Alas, having to bear this burden of uncertainty for another couple of weeks made her feel even more nauseous.

She suddenly felt as though she could not breath. She needed some air, some guidance. She quickly got to her feet, grabbed her jacket and headed out the door to take a walk through the park. She was barely able to swallow the lump in her throat or calm the huge swell of anxiety building in her heart.

It was the latter part of the afternoon in late November. Dusk, darkness descended quite quickly at that time of year in London. As she rounded the Physical Energy statue she noticed, for the first time, the numerous intersected paths in Kensington Gardens and all the various people walking upon them.

Suddenly, it struck Belinda how it all had the likeness of numerous souls walking upon their respective life paths. Belinda watched in wonder as each person continued on a path, some focused, some leisurely and some dazed as if sleepwalking. Some just going forward. Some paused when they arrived at a fork in their path, and were choosing which way to go. Some were distracted by something off their path. And some were stopped in their path as they had encountered someone.

"How utterly fascinating…" she said to herself.

Just then, an amber light in the distance caught her eye. It was one of the park maintenance trucks signaling that the park would soon be closing. She smiled wryly to herself. Belinda and that flashing amber light were old intimate friends. It was one of the first signs she was given. Caution, it had said. Take things slowly, it repeated. If only she had heeded its tacit yet persistent warning she may not have ended up in her current predicament. With a great sigh, she rounded back and headed for the Italian Gardens.

As she approached, a slight shiver caught her and she pulled her tweed newsboy cap lower and drew her navy Pea coat tighter around her body. It had been damp and foggy all afternoon, a lugubrious day, to mimic her despondent mood.

With the impending sunset, the fountains and surrounding trees took on a gloomy, slightly gothic appearance. She sat at her usual bench, on the east side, facing the fountains and closed her eyes. She breathed in deeply, the scent of damp earth and stale fountain water filled her nostrils. She began to rid her mind of any thoughts, focused on her breathing. When she felt calm, still, she silently asked,

"Am I pregnant? "

Belinda opened her eyes and looked straight ahead. The first thing she saw was a tree in the distance. Its silhouette was shrouded in complete darkness against the greying sky, the base surrounded by a dense fog. The tree branches were bare, arching downward, gnarly looking.

Suddenly her gaze was propelled upward, toward the top of the tree. And there it was. Belinda's breath drew in sharply. She blinked a few times, not believing what she was seeing. It was still there. Perched on the very top of the tree was the perfect silhouette of very large bird with two long spindly legs and a very distinctive looking beak.

It sat there, its head turned in profile, taunting Belinda with a perfect view. Could she be mistaken? But, it looked exactly like one. This had to be a horrid joke. She asked Love if she was pregnant and this was the sign she was given? Her heart began to pound. She could not tear her eyes away. In that moment, and she would have sworn her life on it, Belinda was utterly convinced she was staring at the silhouette of none other than a stork.

# Chapter Fourteen

IT HAD BEEN TWO WEEKS SINCE THE STORK INCIDENT. Hitherto Belinda had returned to the Italian Gardens only once for another meditative walk hoping to gain some further guidance or clarity but instead the stork had made yet another torturous appearance.

Truth be told, it was in the distance and partially hidden in the brush but there was no mistaking its silhouette, white plumage and distinctive bill. Belinda had tried to keep it out of her mind. It was just too absurd to believe.

"What you resist, persists." she told herself, "Let it go."

———————

The next day Belinda decided a trip to Portobello Road was in order. She was headed back to Toronto soon and ostensibly wanted to fetch a few unique mementos for her family but ultimately felt the eclectic other worldly charm of Portobello Market would also be a welcome distraction from her current state of mind.

Browsing the numerous stalls was an exercise in restraint, everything appealed to Belinda's erstwhile sensibilities. Heaps of antediluvian jewelry, fox-fur stoles, vintage clothing, leather goods in sumptuous saddle leather and endless sea of silverware were laid out to beguile, to caress and ultimately to purchase.

The saccharine scent of sugar dusted donuts, caramel covered pretzels and candied roasted nuts saturated the air.

She was suddenly transported to the memory of visiting the Exhibition in Toronto as a child. The throngs of people on the road and the sticky, sweet scent in the air made her recall all of the mystery and magical lure of that fair and all the costumes and game booths. The innocent thrill of those times took hold of her. She was swept up, comforted by nostalgia and was suddenly filled with utter bliss. She then forgot her future worries and anxieties, they did not exist in this present moment. She felt the aliveness in her body and with it her connection to Love's presence. And, in that moment of connectedness to Love, all of life was innocent, safe and full of wonder.

---

A little while later Belinda paused at a stall. The table was laden with an impressive collection of Wedgewood china. She scanned the items, adored the unique, whimsical chalky blue and white esthetic. She was about to pick up a tiny jewelry dish when a woman came floating out from behind a heavy, black sheet.

The woman stopped abruptly when she saw Belinda. She had an ageless quality, tilted her head to one side, as she looked Belinda up and down with intense eyes of black jade.

"Yes, that's a lovely piece, but I have something very special for you my darling child…." She disappeared into the back. Belinda glanced around, noticed the street had suddenly become very quiet and dark. The sun had become eclipsed by a dark grey cloud and the bustle of crowds had all gone further down the way leaving her feeling very alone with this curious sorceress-like creature. The woman returned with a tattered red velvet box.

"As soon as I set eyes on you, I knew this piece was meant for you."

The woman smiled, her black jade eyes were heavily smudged with ebony kohl and seemed to peer into Belinda's soul. Her face was deeply tanned, lined with the patina of many years, perhaps many lives. Her hair was hidden, tied up in a gold and black patterned headscarf. Her lips were painted a deep, matte scarlet, the colour bled into the wrinkles around her lips. She had an emerald gemstone in her left nostril and it seemed to gleam like punctuations for her words and gestures. Belinda was a little frightened yet completely bewitched.

The woman opened the red velvet box, removed the item and unwrapped the white tissue paper with flourish. Belinda, barely able to tear her eyes away from this ethereal, gypsy-woman's face, finally glanced at what was in her hands. Her breath quickly drew in, she took a step back, shook her head, grimaced in pain.

Nestled sweetly, amidst a cloud of white tissue, lay the most beautiful, delicate blue egg. It was decoratively etched in white all the way around and centered on the top was a white bird with long thin legs and an all too familiar beak.

"Didn't I tell you it was perfect for you my darling child? As sweet, delicate and nubile as you..."

Belinda was barely able to speak. All she saw was another horrid reminder of her rash behavior and the possibility of her being pregnant.

Alas, Belinda's spirit knew your internal fears, however deeply masked or repressed would always find a way to sublimate, manifest or mirror into your outside reality. You had only to take notice of this coincidence or resonance to recognize a deeper reality was beckoning for reflection, surrender and release.

Unable to speak yet compelled to possess this gorgeous, beastly reminder, she quickly dropped the few pounds it cost onto the table, took the egg in its tissue, shoved it into her purse and without looking at the old woman hurried up the road restraining herself from the nefarious urge of looking back in fear she too just like Lot's wife would be turned to salt for her transgressions.

———••••———

On the walk back to the flat, Belinda cut through Kensington Gardens. She needed to be in nature, be in an open expanse, to breathe the air of sweeping green, earth. She went and sat at the base of a big tree.

Leaning her head back, she closed her eyes. The cold, bumpy hardness of the tree bark against her back centered her, gave her a sense of something strong she could rest against, something of tangible fortitude she could trust and lean on.

What did it all mean? Of all things why did that strange woman give her an egg? Did that gypsy woman know something? Was this a sign that she was indeed pregnant? Her heart needed more time. It was still processing the experience. With a deep, weary sigh she got up and headed for the flat.

Having connected back to Love and the stillness within, Belinda knew that life and its illusions often had you forgetting who you really were. What ensued then was so much needless suffering. Thankfully, she also knew, divine grace would leave loving hints along the way but only if you were present, if you were still enough to see them. Hints that were meant to remind you that we were first and foremost safe, boundless and infinite beings of Love. Beings of Love mistaken in believing that we were just human bodies having isolated experiences that were meant to hurt and cause us pain.

How opposite to truth this was. For while in this world

of form and seeming duality some of the experiences were indeed challenging ones. But there was always a choice. What did she choose? Surely not to be a powerless victim in a mad world. She would always chose truth and the knowing that she was Love. That these challenges were Love's evolutionary lessons, sent from her own soul to keep her awareness of truth growing. And each choice was a choice to awaken to who you really were and remind yourself that only Love was real.

---

The next day the sun was shining brilliantly. Belinda opened the bedroom window, beckoned the new day, the sun and the light in. A new day warranted a fresh start, a new outlook. And yet, undeniably, yesterday's entire ordeal brought to the forefront many thoughts on her current path.

Belinda headed to the kitchen to put on a pot of tea, further putting off what she knew waited. She sat at the kitchen table, chin in her hand, looking out the window onto Pimlico Road. Across the street there were two tradesmen working at refurbishing the façade of a shop. One on either side, both punctiliously scrapping away, by hand, years and layers of soot, paint and varnish and slowly but surely revealing the building's inner glory – a tile of the most exquisite deep indigo blue.

Alas, like so much of humankind, Belinda mused, so many of us walking around covered up with layers and layers of pain, negativity and suffering that we've ultimately forgotten who we really are and how marvelous and grand our inner being really was. Belinda continued to observe them and surrendered to the desire for contemplation.

She had set out on this journey to write her first book and she had for the most part achieved that goal. Oddly, she just needed the end; something that completed the circle of experiences and with it imparted the profound and ultimate lesson or insight. But as of yet, it continued to elude her.

She knew being in London felt truly wonderful. She knew in her heart that she was meant to come here and experience all that she had, even as anguish-filled and confusing as many parts of this journey had been to endure.

Regardless, she was consciously nurturing a sense of gratitude for all of it; her creativity and writing, the Fellow and their romantic whirlwind and gratitude also for the heart-wrenching decision to go their separate ways. Belinda was determined to see all of it as loving, evolutionary lessons on her path. But, the most challenging and life altering lesson would be revealed very shortly. She took a few conscious breaths. She knew she could not put it off any longer and rose from the table.

A few minutes later she was seated on the edge of her bed, trying to resolve that whatever the outcome was she would trust that this moment was as it should be. Whatever happened she would be able to handle it, come what may. Just as the thought passed through her head, the timer went off alerting her that the two minutes were up. She stood and walked slowly, with her head held high, into the loo. She was suddenly very calm, a comforting peace swept over her as she picked up the pregnancy test, and with a steady hand, turned it over.

Staring at her was the clearest sign she'd been given to date. There was no mistaking its meaning. She sat down on the lavatory lid, staring at the slender, white, plastic wand. The result was negative. Belinda felt a pastiche of conflicting emotions engulf her. Relief. Joy. Sadness. Disappointment.

How could it be? It didn't make any sense dammit. Why on earth had she been feeling so nauseous, so fatigued? For weeks no less and then the stork sign in the park? Not once but twice. What, pray tell, was that about?

She felt like she was going mad. She suddenly hated all the signs, the ambiguity of life. Why couldn't everything just be simple, be clear? She knew she was mostly frustrated with herself, the fact that she was at a very ambivalent stage in her life. Coming to London had taken a lot of courage. Had it all been for naught? Right now she didn't feel very much ahead from when she first set out on this journey, in terms of insight, her true Love or true path for that matter. All she had wanted was a bit of guidance, just enough to let her know she was at least heading in the right direction. Was that too much to ask? Belinda felt very humbled and resigned to the fact that she would never have life all figured out. No one would. The moment anyone thought they had life figured out, life would surely swoop in and lovingly remind you otherwise. She knew she would forever be life's humble pupil, one who still had a lot to unlearn rather than learn. Frustrated, she snapped the wand in half.

# Chapter Fifteen

BELINDA ZIPPED UP HER SUITCASE AND LIFTED IT UPRIGHT onto the floor. She could not help but notice that the suitcase's enormous weight was much less cumbersome then when she had arrived. She smiled, a knowing smile, understood that somehow things had come full circle.

She was leaving London later that day and she had to admit she was quite pleased with herself. The week prior she had finished the first draft of her manuscript. The entire stork and pregnancy imbroglio had galvanized her to re-frame the situation, recognize the lessons which in turn guided her to take the moment by the reins, become a co-creator in this beautiful, uncertain, sometimes messy yet always exhilarating Love story that was unfolding around her.

With this illumined vision she managed to finish the creative challenge that had inspired this journey from the onset and it was beyond gratifying. She recalled the day she had typed her last sentence. She had pushed back from the table with a certainty in her heart that this chapter, this brilliant, tumultuous, joyous chapter in London was now nearing completion.

Most importantly she knew, without a doubt, that she wanted to go home. No, she was ready to go home. Belinda realized she had never felt that way before. The thought of *home* had never had such a strong and visceral pull. Going home had never felt as right as it did in that moment. Home to where her family, her friends and her life steadfastly waited for her with open, loving arms.

Through her personal explorations and experiences in London and ultimately writing this journey down she had found her way back to the beginning, back to her homeland and to the home in her heart. T.S Eliot, one of the twentieth centuries major poets knew this insight and elegantly shared it with the rest of us in his poem Little Giddings:

> *We shall not cease from exploration, and the end of*
> *all our exploring will be to arrive where we started*
> *and know the place for the first time.*

So much out ward and in ward exploration, only to find herself where it all began, peacefully ensconced back in her own heart. Who was it also that said, that the best journey in life was always the journey home? Never before had those words resonated as profoundly as they did with Belinda right now.

The fact that her book's story was taken from her own current life story felt like, perhaps, it may have been the whole point all along. Looking back at the trajectory of emotions and events on this adventure Belinda could see how her path first began with a yearning to re-connect with her own creative spirit, which in turn had inspired her to take herself out of her comfort zone and depart to London. It was a yearning so deep and so profound that it transcended many of her egotistic attachments to the emotional and material comforts of her elegant life and flat in Toronto. Her creative spirit's pull was so strong that it enabled her to walk away from it all without a second thought or glance.

> *Be in this world but not of it.*

She finally understood what that verse truly meant. Her path had then collided with the Fellow's and she could now see how she had so easily and so unmindfully abandoned her own path to explore the foreign allure of an experience with him. Another one of Love's evolutionary lesson's to see how devoted one was to their destiny. Thankfully, her openness to Love's truth had gracefully caused Belinda to finally see the signs, the tiny pearls of knowledge dotted along the way to help guide her back to her true path. In stillness and trust she was able to re-trace her steps, bring herself back to her truth.

For our spirit and true path was always there, waiting patiently, yet always gently beckoning for our return. Were all of Love's lessons simply that, seductive detours to test our faith and commitment to our soul's grand agenda, she wondered? All of those lessons came as unexpected yet profound insights, now forever etched in her heart.

Yet, the final denouement of this London story, that somehow pulled it all together, still eluded her. Regardless, she knew in her heart that as long as she stayed true to the creative and heroic within her, trusted her heart, her creative spirit as her guiding compass and recognized the tests, detours along the way she would indeed always walk smoothly and swiftly towards her destiny

She glanced at her watch; there was just enough time to do two last vital things. She reached into her pocket, feeling for the slip of paper. Yes, it was still there. She slipped on her trench coat, tweed cap and headed out the door. Once outside, she lifted her head aloft and let the sun warm her face. Who said the sun never shone in London? It was the most brilliant day and her blithe, open heart was feeling equally as brilliant.

The sun was radiant, a throbbing expanse in a cloudless azure sky. Both seemed to be bearing themselves and their perfect truth to Belinda. Nature was constantly exposing its emotions, its tenderness, ferocity and truth to all of us. Thus always encouraging us to do the same. Come, it seemed to say, just as you are and join in the revelry, the wonder of just being alive. Being one with Love. Share in the unadulterated wonder, beauty and grace that was our divine birthright. It was in those moments that she felt that her veins and natures veins were inextricably connected, fused with the same flow, the same life force that coursed through them, ultimately leading to a universal beating heart.

Belinda wasn't sure when the turning point had occurred or if it had just been a culmination of all the events and repetition of signs and symbols over the past few months that had made everything crystallize with such clarity. But she knew a new process had begun, a process of letting go of certain beliefs and values that no longer served her, that transcended the ego's noetic pull. A process that would continue to show her first that she truly was the hero of her own life story and that the devotion to her creative spirit within and it's all-seeing vision for her life was at the heart of each of our Love stories. It seemed so simple.

So much of Taoist teachings conveyed this, and one in particular came to mind for her;

> *"I have just three things to teach: simplicity, patience and compassion. These three things are your greatest treasures. Simple in actions and in thoughts, one returns to the source of being"*

Resting in these simply pointers to truth, she would find herself on her way to hearing the hearts subtle yet powerful urgings to engage and nurture that tremendous silent witness, one's essence.

This universal truth was the most certain thing in life. Love and all of its equal parts: timelessness, innocence, beauty, compassion, creativity, abundance, flexibility, integrity, surrender and playfulness comprised a full, passionate life and ensured depth and meaning to your life and journey. One's connection to that source was the secret to a life truly lived and expressed.

Belinda knew, without a doubt, that nurturing her connection with her own creative spirit and ultimately increasing her awareness of truth within would keep her on the path and enable her to see the Love story that was unfolding *right now* before her very eyes and not in some distant future. *Love was here now.* For, she was Love. We all were. All she needed was willingness and an unwavering resolve to trust Love's guidance and commune with it daily.

The fact that her life right now was whole, interdependent, meaning-full and purpose-filled according to how she chose to give it meaning and purpose was a divine truth and a liberation that could only come directly from Love. She knew surrendering to her creative spirits path and trusting it's unfolding was a call she was finally ready to humbly accept. No seeking or veering off her path was necessary. Every opportunity or person meant for her would meet her on her path and flow with it, not disconnect her from Love or take her off her path. All she had to do was yield to Love's process. Get out of her own way to realize her soul's grandest potential, a potential that her limited human view and ego desperately wanted to control. Knowing and recognizing the difference was the ultimate challenge.

A challenge she now relished.

Belinda set off for the park, feeling exhilarated by the joy coursing through her veins. Kensington Gardens was alive, vibrant with children frolicking, people happily walking and seated couples of all ages embracing. As she entered the Italian Gardens she stopped to take a visual snapshot of this otherworldly place. With the water garden's ethereal beauty before her, the beaming sun mingled with the sound and spray of the fountains rushing water Belinda felt herself transported to a different moment in time. A place where the symphony of life played out and her past, present and future were all happening now simultaneously, joyously and culminating in a brilliant crescendo called Love.

She headed past the Italian Gardens, down Long Water to the little alcove where Peter Pan held court. She stood before him, his impish stance eternally playful, his childlike face perpetually smiling. She reached inside her pocket and took out the piece of paper. It was fashioned into the shape of a heart and in the center she had written the Fellow's name. She took a few deep conscious breaths and closed her eyes.

Belinda silently, with her entire being sent thanks to Love. She thanked Love for bringing him into her life and all the lessons and insights she had learnt about herself and her journey through their communion. She then sent the Fellow eternal gratitude for the beautiful, spiritual and evolutionary experience they had shared. She finally sent him Love; peaceful, joyful and blissful Love. Love emanated from every part of her, it was a sparkling white light that imbued her heart and shone out into the universes consciousness. She then, finally, silently, peacefully, let him go.

Belinda had never known such sweet surrender, such utter freedom. She then made a vow, a vow to herself. She vowed, just like Peter Pan, that she too would always honour the heroic child in herself. She promised to never forget the importance of nurturing innocence and wonder and playfulness in all things.

She opened her eyes, folded the heart in half and

scanned the statue. She saw the perfect spot, a tiny crevice between two dancing fairies. She tucked the note snugly between them, trusted they would take her message where it needed to go.

Belinda walked back to the Italian Gardens, marveled at how this place had become such an intimate friend, an oasis and her own personal Oracle of Delphi.

*Know Thyself.* These were the famous words inscribed above the entrance to the temple of Apollo at Delphi, the original site of the sacred Oracle in Greece where centuries ago people would flock to the Oracle in hopes of gleaning what their destiny was to be or the answer to a personal quandary. The words *Know Thyself* encouraged them to seek out their own personal truth but it was also, she felt, the Oracle's way of pointing to the deeper truth; the universal truth that all answers are never to be found outside oneself but always and only within oneself. A truth that was, ironically, revealed by simply switching those to inscribed words around: *Thyself Know.*

Belinda smiled to herself as she entered the gardens, taking in its romantic splendor. She was not only here to bid it farewell but also to express her deep and eternal gratitude for all its patience and sagacious guidance.

She was compelled to walk to the south end of the water gardens that overlook Long Water. She approached the concrete balustrade and peered out. She closed her eyes and took a deep breath, filling her lungs with the cool, crisp February air. Opening her eyes, she knew the stillness of the water reflected the stillness in her heart.

Suddenly, off to her right, something white caught her eye. She turned her head, gasped and then burst out into laughter. There, on a rock protruding from the water gallantly stood her stork. She shook her head in sheer amazement. Finally, it all made sense. Utter, divine and ludicrous sense. This last, grand revelation was the elusive piece to her journey's puzzle. Standing before her, in all of its calm, dignified splendor was not a stork at all but a Great Blue Heron. She smiled wryly to herself. And, of course, this life altering epiphany had to be delivered by an English Heron, no less.

Belinda watched the bird in complete awe. Perhaps sensing her intense admiration, the heron turned its head and peered right back at her. They were now both gazing at each other, and for a moment she felt they were one, two spirits recognizing and paying homage to the other. *Namaste.*

The symbolism of the Great Blue Heron and its appearance in her life right now was abundantly clear to Belinda. It was widely known in many wisdom traditions that the heron was revered for its many hero-like qualities; integrity, grace, independence, patience, self-determination, purity and dedication to one's path in life, to name a few.

Their long thin legs were also symbols. Symbols of balance, for the longer the legs the deeper the water the heron would wade and feed in and the deeper life could be explored. *Know Thyself.* Their frail looking legs were also a reminder to Belinda that she did not require massive pillars to remain strong, stable and independent on her path. That fortitude came from within. The heron, heralded by mystic sages for its innate wisdom, was also an emblem to demonstrate that if she were truly dedicated to living her dreams she could sublimate her hearts desires into this reality.

Belinda recalled the first time the heron had appeared in her life. She had been fraught with such enormous anxiety over the possibility of being pregnant she had mistaken its darkened silhouette for that of a stork and in true Dante-esque fashion descended to her own *Inferno* the days that followed. Alas, where had her Virgil been, to soothe and guide her through that treacherous psychological terrain? Then, seeing the bird again two weeks later partially hidden in the lake's brush she again mistook it for a stork. Her heart having survived the initial inexorable shock and anguish felt no comfort, as a life doomed to eternal reflection of her unconscious actions in *Purgatorio* seemed her only destiny. Yet today, there was no mistaking anything. Just as her mind and heart were calm and connected to truth, so too was the heron's identity and meaning in her life. And with this realization she, just like Dante was granted ascension to Love and *Paradiso*. Belinda laughed aloud to herself. Life truly was a *Divine Comedy*. A comedy where;

*Love's signs didn't get louder, they only get clearer.*

It was true; if she was still and calm in the present moment all of life's answers were right there within her. Her heart had been trying to tell her that very thing over and over again but she had not been willing or ready to see it. She took comfort in the fact that Love, forever faithful to one on their path, would continue to gently, lovingly prod her towards awakening to the truth within her. Belinda knew that in order to remain true to Love all she ever needed to do was turn inward, commune with Love, be still and heed Love's universal scope and wisdom and let it guide her in peace to where she was meant to go.

And ultimately, beyond any romantic relationship, the connection and sacred relationship she had with the Love within her directly equated to the amount of Love she experienced in her outer life. Belinda saw how this truly required a letting go and an unwavering trust in Love and its all-seeing vision and guidance in her life. Belinda knew when she truly surrendered, truly let go and watched without attachment or expectation the natural unfolding and rhythm of her life over the promptings of others, society or anything else that appeared along the way she would always be guided to soar with magnificence, just like the Great Blue Heron, towards her sacred truth and the life she was meant to live right now, the life of her dreams.

It's that simple, truly.